SIDE EFFECTS

•

Mel and Karen Silverstein

DOUBLEDAY & COMPANY, INC.
GARDEN CITY, NEW YORK
1978

All of the characters in this book are fictitious, and any resemblance to actual persons, living or dead, is purely coincidental.

ISBN: 0-385-13632-3
Library of Congress Catalog Card Number 77-92231

COPYRIGHT © 1978 BY M. J. SILVERSTEIN, M.D. AND
K. J. SILVERSTEIN
ALL RIGHTS RESERVED
PRINTED IN THE UNITED STATES OF AMERICA
FIRST EDITION

*To the men and women of today
who are struggling to get through any crisis
and are learning to love each other.*

SIDE EFFECTS

ACKNOWLEDGMENTS

For their continuing comments, ideas, support and love we want to thank Milton and Margit Sperling; Louis and Jeanette Silverstein; Lenore, Cheryl and Debbie Aisoff.

For providing us with a wonderful place to work, a Xerox machine and especially unlimited encouragement, thoughts and love, we want to thank Betty and Stanley Sheinbaum.

And finally, we want to thank the two people who believed in us from the very beginning: Helen Barrett, our agent at William Morris; and Kate Medina, our wise and patient editor at Doubleday.

SIDE EFFECTS

1

Five or six men were standing to the side of court ten. "Jesus Christ! Look at those tits bounce!" one of them said.

A soft shot came over the net and Cynthia Rogers smashed it back at the feet of her opponent. "Forty-fifteen," she announced, as she walked back to the base line.

Her body was hard and muscular and tan. She wore a crocheted low-cut one-piece tennis dress. She had large beautifully shaped breasts that moved up and down and side to side every time she took a step. The faster she moved, the more her breasts moved. The only time she wore a bra was when she played tennis and that was because she was a serious tennis player.

Cynthia threw the ball high in the air and hit a surprisingly hard serve for a woman. Her opponent just got it back. Cynthia smashed the return to her backhand. Her opponent, outclassed, just managed to get her racket on the ball, hitting a high shot that landed on the base line. Cynthia watched closely as the ball fell.

"Out!" she yelled. "That's the game and the match."

"Are you sure that was out?" her opponent called back.

"Yes," Cynthia said, as she headed toward the net to shake hands with the other woman.

"It was in," one of the men whispered.

"Who gives a damn," another man said, "she'd win anyway, and I don't care how the hell she wins. I just like watching her move."

A third man turned to the others. "I've always wondered what a woman who looks like that feels when I'm talking to her and I can't take my eyes off her body."

Cynthia wiped the sweat off the back of her neck as she headed toward the clubhouse. She liked to win. Winning had been one of the few ways she'd found to please her father.

2

Jon Meyer reached over the edge of the bed and, without looking, he found the small oblong gray box. As he picked it up, his index finger pressed the little black button on one end and the noise coming from it stopped. He placed the silenced beeper on the end table and turned over to face the other side of the bed. "Can I use the phone?"

"Sure," she answered. As she leaned over and reached for the phone, Meyer noticed a small darkly pigmented lesion on her lower back.

"Don't turn around a second." He flipped the light on above the bed and took a closer look.

"What's wrong?"

"I'm just looking at a mole." He rubbed his finger across it and then looked even closer. "It's nothing." And he patted her naked buttocks.

She smiled. "How much do I owe you?"

"For the examination, nothing."

She handed him the phone and he dialed. "This is Dr. Meyer. . . . Sure, put him through. Hi, Jerry. What's up?" He listened intently for a few moments. He was clearly disturbed by whatever he was hearing. "That's a shame. Is his wife there? . . . Good. Keep her there. I want to speak to her. Tell her I'm on my way . . . thirty minutes, or so." And he hung up. "I've got to go."

"What's the matter?"

"A nice young woman's husband died." He stood up and walked into the bathroom.

"The man is going to die," the professor had said. "The cancer has won and we have lost. There is little we can do for him other than to make his last days comfortable." The verdict had been pronounced and there was no appeal.

Jon Meyer had seen that first cancer patient in 1958 when he was a sophomore in medical school. Cancer patients were certainly not the reason he had decided to become a doctor. Why should he bother to try to treat the untreatable? He had wanted to be a great physician, a savior. He had wanted to help people, not stand idly by while disease ran an unchecked incurable course.

"Jon," she yelled into the bathroom. "When will I see you again?"

He dried his face. "Soon."

The care of the cancer patient: what a depressing and unrewarding field, he remembered thinking. If anyone had said then that years later it would be his only total commitment in life, he would have said that they were crazy.

She came to the door of the bathroom and stood there, naked. "What does 'soon' mean?"

"It means, soon . . . when we both feel like it again." He finished dressing, kissed her on the cheek and left.

Each time a patient died, no matter how many times he had been through it, he always had a variety of feelings to sort out. He hated to lose a patient. Why had he chosen a field in which it was so difficult to win?

By the time he was a senior in medical school, he had decided to become a surgeon. It was an exciting field with immediate gratification and Meyer was basically impatient. He couldn't wade through four or five dates before he went to bed with a girl and he couldn't stand the thought of becoming an internist and treating heart patients with digitalis for two or three years without any real results.

When a knife wound or a gunshot wound of the abdomen came in, he rushed the patient to the operating room and fixed the damage. Nothing was more exciting. Step right up, three doctors, no waiting. Meyer the surgeon versus the clock and death. It was playing God.

The forty-two-year-old gall bladder down the hall, you know, the fat lady in 315. Meyer took out her gall bladder. A week later she went home and a week after that she was eating bacon every morning and growing fatter—but now, without pain! The gall bladder was out and the disease was cured. But what about the patient? She was cured, wasn't she? Her pain was gone. But why did she eat so much, Dr. Meyer? Was she unhappy? "I don't know. I never asked." Does she still make it with her husband? "I don't know that either. I'm a surgeon. I just took out her gall bladder. I'm not a goddamn psychiatrist!"

The impersonal environment of the surgical world with its artificial dissociation of person and disease seemed completely normal and appropriate to Meyer. It had taken Nancy three years to convince him that it wasn't.

Meyer slipped out the garage door behind the apartment building and stepped into his silver Porsche. It had been an extravagance when he first bought it in 1970, but now it was just a wonderful old car that he loved. And he took good care of it.

He sped down the freeway toward the hospital.

When they were first married, Nancy was a sweet little girl who wanted to be a wife, a mother and a physician in that order. Meyer was a big, strong, arrogant surgical resident who fucked lots of women and saved lots of lives. He had proudly announced that he loved surgery more than anything else and always would. He was afraid to love anything else, particularly Nancy.

Nancy was a psychiatric resident when she married Meyer. She talked about disease while he did something about it; that was his favorite joke. Surgery cured people: he cut out the sickness and the patient got well.

He had taken Nancy on rounds often, but only to impress her with what he had done. "This is my wife, the other Dr. Meyer." And he would smile. "Do you mind if we take a look at your incision?" The patient, that time, was a forty-nine-year-old woman who had been the first upon whom Meyer had performed a radical mastectomy and he was very proud. So there would be some degree of privacy, he had pulled the curtains around her bed, but he hadn't completely closed them.

She'd sat quietly on her bed, her left breast moving as she breathed. On the right side of her chest was a long vertical scar stretching from her lower ribs to her shoulder. The stitches holding the wound together were still in place and becoming red. The skin was stretched tightly over the ribs, which were easily visible. The depression beneath the collarbone, where the muscle had been removed, was grotesque.

"It's beautiful," Meyer had said. "The wound is healing well. There's no fluid beneath the skin flaps. It's a great result." He'd looked at the patient and then back at his wife. "All the lymph nodes in her axilla were negative. That means she's probably cured." He was so pleased. It was another surgical triumph.

The woman had looked at Meyer and then at Nancy. She'd hesitated, then she'd said, "It's ugly, isn't it?" And she'd begun to cry.

Nancy had covered her up. She'd taken her hand and sat down beside her. "It isn't pretty and it'll never be the same, but in time it'll look better. Jon"—she'd turned to him—"why don't you finish rounds and let us women talk for a while."

And he'd finally realized it. He wasn't the total physician. He needed to learn to listen to patients, to understand their feelings, to understand what they were going through and to treat their emotions as well as their bodies. But when it came time to be giving and understanding on a personal level, he continued to fail. And after his divorce, Meyer seldom took the time to get personally involved with anyone for very long.

Deciding to become a surgeon was a decision Meyer had made on his own. Deciding to get divorced was a decision he had made with Nancy. And deciding to devote his medical life to bettering the care of cancer patients was a decision he would never have made had he not known and lived with a person like Nancy.

He pulled into the hospital parking lot and headed toward the large gray building.

3

Cynthia opened the front door and let Jerry Roberts into her apartment. He removed his short white doctor's coat and sat down heavily on the couch in the living room. He had been on call for the last day and a half and he was tired.

"Want a drink?" Cynthia offered.

"Haven't got time, today." He smiled. "I've got to get home in an hour."

She stood in the doorway of her kitchen, not really wanting to come into the room. "I've changed my mind," she sighed.

"What are you talking about?"

"Just what I said," she looked at him. "No more."

"Then why did you have me drive all the way out here? I could have gone straight home from the hospital." Jerry scanned Cynthia's body as she leaned against the doorjamb. He wanted her. "What's the matter with you? You've been acting strangely for the last month."

"Jerry . . . you're married."

"So what. You've known that all along."

"It's just not right for me anymore . . . no more . . . I've been doing a lot of thinking lately."

She was just too beautiful not to try. "Come on, Cynthia," he drawled. "Sit down." He patted the seat next to him. "Let's talk about this." He looked up at her and broke into a winning smile.

She didn't smile back as she shook her head. "No, thanks, Jerry. I meant what I said."

"You know it's a goddamn long ride out here," he said. "Why didn't you just tell me over the phone?"

Cynthia turned away and then she turned back and walked over to him. She did owe him some sort of an explanation. She'd been dissatisfied with her life for the past year, she'd wanted to make some changes, but somehow she hadn't done much about it until this moment. She sat down on the couch next to him.

"Jerry, you were a safe relationship. I really couldn't get involved with you, nor could you with me. Now, I just don't want to be with people anymore who are unavailable and who can't really care for me."

Jerry moved closer, slipping his arm around her shoulder. "I do care for you. You know that."

"That's not really the point." And she leaned forward, almost out of his grasp. Something had finally clicked. She was doing something she should have done months ago. There would be no more inaccessible people in her life. No more men like her father. Her father had failed her after her mother's death, by not being available, by giving her everything but love. And she'd failed him, too, by not using what he gave her to amount to more in her own life. But Jerry wasn't going to be interested in any of that. She needed to tell him something he could understand.

"You're being silly," he said, as he moved his arm forward and around her shoulder again. "We're good together."

She sat back, moving away from him. He put his hand up to her blond head and brushed the wisps of soft hair away from her face.

"You're beautiful," he continued. He knew he could win her back, he'd done it with others.

"I've decided," she said firmly. "It's just better for me not to go out with you or anyone else who's unavailable. Can't you understand that? Unavailable means that you can't really make a commitment to someone else. I want a different kind of relationship."

Jerry dropped his hand. "Who'd you meet?"

"I haven't met anyone. I don't know anyone like that." She had to force herself to change now. No more Jerry and no more men like Jerry.

He leaned toward her and cupped her breast in his hand, gently stroking it like an admirer of a fine piece of sculptured marble.

She sat there silently, letting him.

"One more time," Jerry pleaded. "Just once more, so I can remember your beautiful body."

She pushed him away, angrily. "You haven't heard a word that I've said. Jerry, you're a doctor," she said softly, "you have to learn to listen to people. Someday one of them will need you."

What more could he do or say? He'd tried. She'd gotten him all the way out here and she'd wasted his time. He reached over and took her by the shoulders, then he slid his hands down her sides to her waist. He held her for a moment trying to think of something to say. "That lump still there?"

She nodded, yes. He'd taken her off guard and she delayed in pulling away. He seized the opportunity and began to knead her flesh, moving closer to her, thinking she might change her mind.

She pulled away and stood up quickly.

"I thought you were going to refer me to a doctor."

"Sure," he said.

She walked farther away from him. "Who will you recommend?"

Jerry Roberts stood up abruptly. "What the fuck does it matter? He's just going to check those big tits of yours."

And he walked out of Cynthia's apartment, slamming the door behind him.

4

Meyer pulled down the upper gastrointestinal X rays that were hanging on the view box and put up a single chest film in their place.

"Not bad, Larry," he said. "You put that case together very well."

If there was a single academic pursuit that Meyer loved, it was teaching. He enjoyed giving medical students, interns and residents all that he knew, watching them accept what they believed and reject what they didn't. He looked at the chest X ray on the view box. "All right, Ann. Tell me everything you can about this patient."

Ann looked at him and smiled. She was glad that he had called on her. Two weeks ago the same type of exercise almost had her in tears. She wasn't the only one, though. At first the other students were also intimidated by having to participate in Meyer's aggressive teaching sessions. But they quickly learned that he never bit anyone's head off even when he threatened it.

Ann very carefully looked at the X ray. "Well, it's a man about forty-five years old. The heart is normal. The lung fields are clear." She hesitated and looked even more closely, searching for some abnormality. "The bones and soft tissues look normal." She smiled uneasily. She knew very well that Dr. Jon Meyer did not put up normal chest X rays for his students' evaluation. She looked at the film a final time, then turned and faced Meyer. She shrugged her shoulders. "It looks okay to me."

"You all agree with Ann?" Meyer asked, smiling.

The other medical students taking the oncology elective nodded their heads passively, their way of admitting that they hadn't spotted the hidden pathology either.

"You're all wrong. This patient is forty years old, so you're right about the age, but he's a she!"

"He's a she?" Ann repeated, disbelievingly.

"That's what I just said. This is the chest X ray of a female patient, not a male. What made you so certain that it was a man?"

Ann looked closely at the X ray again. "There are no breasts here," she said. "This patient is obviously an adult. You can tell that by looking at the bones. And adult women have shadows caused by their breasts that you can see right here." She pointed to the middle of the X ray. "And this patient doesn't have them."

"So because you didn't see any breast shadows on the X ray, you assumed that it was a male?"

"Of course," Ann said.

"Ninety-nine times out of a hundred, you'd be right, but today you're wrong. This is a female patient without breasts and there are a couple of subtle clues on the film that might have suggested it." And Meyer began pointing them out.

"Every time you see a chest X ray that looks like this, you're going to have to consider that possibility. It's a rare one, but you're going to have to consider it. If you don't, you won't be worth a damn as a doctor."

"How stupid . . ." Ann said.

Meyer interrupted. "It's not stupid, Ann. It's a mistake that just about everyone makes. What I'm trying to show the four of you is the trouble you can get into by jumping to conclusions, by making definitive statements before you know all the facts. I can fool you ten times a day like this. What you've got to learn is not to let me, or the National Board of Medical Examiners, or anyone else put one over on you. If you're going to become good physicians, you're going to have to watch every detail. Now answer the question, Ann. Under what circumstances do we see an adult female without breasts?"

Ann looked at him. "Congenital reasons . . . perhaps this patient was born without breast tissue, or if she had breast tissue it was never stimulated by the proper hormones."

"That's reasonable, but, of course, highly unlikely," Meyer replied. "What about acquired causes?"

"Well, trauma and cancer come to mind."

"Which would be a more common cause for a problem like this one?" he asked.

"Trauma is very common," Ann said, "but I doubt that a woman loses both breasts very often due to a car accident or something like that."

"I agree," Meyer said. "So you think cancer of both breasts would be the most common cause for this clinical picture?"

All the students nodded.

"I agree too. About six per cent of the ninety thousand

women with new cases of breast cancer each year go on to develop a second cancer in the opposite breast. So that makes about five thousand cases a year. Bilateral breast cancer is uncommon but it certainly happens. Think of it next time!"

Meyer frowned as he looked at his watch. It was 1:15 and he was late. "All right, we'll meet on 6-North at five o'clock for rounds."

Meyer gathered his papers together, left the conference room and headed down the hall toward his office.

Jerry Roberts, one of his most conscientious residents, stopped him. "Dr. Meyer, can I talk with you for a second?"

"Sure, Jerry. What's on your mind?"

"Would you do me a favor?" He hesitated for a moment, seeming almost embarrassed. "Would you see someone for me . . . with a small lump in her breast?"

"Your wife?"

"No, just a friend."

Meyer smiled, immediately setting him at ease. "I'd be glad to. Just arrange it with my secretary."

"Thank you. By the way, her name is Cynthia Rogers."

5

Cynthia Rogers went to see Meyer a few days after Jerry Roberts had made the appointment for her.

She was tall, about five feet eight, with straight, thick blondish hair. She wore no make-up and no bra. Her clothes were tight-fitting and expensive-looking.

Meyer's first thought, as he looked at her, was that her breasts were too big to go unsupported. That was his medical point of view. From all other points of view, he thought it was fine.

As she crossed the room, he stood and extended his hand. Not a word had been exchanged, yet he found himself excited by this person.

"Hi, I'm Dr. Meyer." And he smiled at her.

She shook his hand with a much firmer grip than he'd expected. "Hello, I'm Cynthia Rogers, Jerry Roberts' friend." She sat down and straightened her skirt.

Meyer opened the blank chart and picked out a pencil from his top drawer. "I'm glad to meet you. Jerry told me that he found a small lump in your breast."

She nodded, yes. "The right one."

"How long has it been there?"

"I'm not really sure . . . a few weeks or so."

"How big is it?"

"It's small." She held up two slender fingers with about a half inch of space between them.

"What does it feel like?"

"I can't always feel it. When I can, it's like a little marble."

Her eyes were a deep blue and Meyer found himself staring at her. "Has the lump changed at all since you've been examining it or with your menstrual cycle?" Meyer caught himself. That was probably a stupid question. She could hardly feel the lump and since she'd only known about it for a couple of weeks, the odds were that she hadn't even had a menstrual period yet.

"I'm just about due for my period . . . in a few days."

"Before you knew about this lump, did you ever examine your own breasts?"

She shook her head and shrugged. "Not really."

"Why not?"

"I don't know. I guess I never really wanted to find anything."

"You know the earlier you find something the more treatable it is."

She nodded her head in agreement.

"Have you injured your breasts recently?"

"I play a lot of tennis and dance. I guess they get banged around all the time." She smiled. "But, no, I haven't injured them."

Meyer looked carefully into her eyes again. They were large and sensitive. What a perfect-looking woman, he thought. She was absolutely his style. What the hell was she doing running around with a married resident?

"How old are you?" Meyer asked as he stared at her date of birth in the right-hand corner of her chart.

"Twenty-eight."

"Are your parents alive?"

A sad look came across her face and she shook her head, no.

"Neither of them?" Meyer asked softly.

"No. My father died a few years ago of a heart attack and my mother died"—she hesitated—"when I was twelve. She had breast cancer."

"I'm sorry," Meyer said. "Has anyone else in the family ever had cancer?"

"No, not to my knowledge." She quickly regained her composure and smiled at him.

"What medicines do you take?"

"Nothing special, vitamins, aspirin for an occasional headache, and birth-control pills."

"Anything else?"

"No."

"How long have you been on birth-control pills?"

"Seven or eight years."

That was a long time to be on the pill, he thought. And he wondered whether she was promiscuous. What the hell was he thinking? A young woman came to him as a patient. What right did he have to judge her private life?

He completed taking her history and then he pushed the intercom button and asked his nurse to take her into the examining room.

Meyer remained seated at his desk, not looking at any other charts. It was the first time that he had ever been so physically aware of a patient. This woman was beautiful.

But it was more than that. There was something about her, something that fascinated him.

Meyer got up from his desk and walked toward the examining room. For him, examining bodies was a routine nonsexual experience. Out of all the countless women he'd examined since he'd become a doctor, not one of them had ever had the initial effect on him that this woman seemed to have. He stopped outside the examining room door. Something was unsettling to him about these thoughts. At thirty-eight his life was as orderly and disciplined as he could make it. There was little room for any confused feelings, especially about just one person; there were enough people who depended on him right here in the hospital and he liked it that way.

He opened the door.

Cynthia sat on the edge of the examining table. She was wrapped in two sheets: one from her waist down and the other covering the front of her upper body and tucked under her arms.

Meyer examined her head and neck, taking almost more time than necessary.

Finally, he removed the upper sheet, stepped back and looked at her breasts. They were large and beautifully shaped. Their curves were gentle, round, soft and sweeping. Her breasts were firm and full and there was little space between them. They didn't hang down pendulously like one might expect breasts of this size to do. Rather, they came out from her chest, almost defying gravity. Her skin was perfectly smooth and her breasts were completely brown and sun-tanned like the rest of her body.

She had the most magnificent body that he had ever

seen. Even as he thought this, he was cautioning himself against making such an observation. Whatever else she had or was, she was still his patient and that had to remain uppermost in his mind.

He had her move her arms in a variety of directions as he looked for skin changes or lumps that might be visible only in certain positions.

Each time he looked into her eyes, she looked right back at him. At one point they both smiled.

She continued sitting on the edge of the table as he began to palpate her breasts, her nipples becoming erect as soon as he touched her.

She blushed. "I'm sorry."

Meyer's nurse, who was in the room with them, frowned, showing obvious displeasure. He completed the breast examination with Cynthia lying flat on the table.

Jerry Roberts had been right. She had a small lump about one centimeter in diameter, located deep in the upper outer quadrant of the right breast. It was smooth, freely movable and nontender. Meyer made a mental note to compliment Jerry Roberts. He deserved an "A" in physical diagnosis, and an "F" in marriage.

"Jerry was right," Meyer said.

Cynthia forced a smile. She'd wanted him to be wrong.

The rest of her physical examination revealed a perfectly healthy twenty-eight-year-old woman. He taught her how to do breast self-examination and made certain that she could feel the lump.

Meyer went back into his office as Cynthia dressed. As he sat waiting for her to return, he couldn't help thinking about her. She was certainly the most physically appealing woman he had ever seen. He wondered what kind of a person she was and he was sorry that he had met her under these circumstances. He would have much preferred to have met her somewhere else, anywhere else, as long as it was outside the hospital.

Cynthia finished straightening her skirt as she came back into his office. She smiled and sat down.

"You have a very small lump, not even a half inch in diameter."

She nodded her head.

"I don't think it's anything significant."

"By significant, what do you mean?"

"I don't think it's cancer," he continued in an official tone, "I think it's a benign tumor that we call a fibroadenoma. If that's what it is, it'll have to be removed, because in general they don't go away."

"All right." There was no fear or concern in her eyes and Meyer liked that. She was brave and she understood what probably had to be done.

But Cynthia was an expert at not showing her feelings. After her mother had died, she'd learned that all that interested her father was his work and a happy-looking daughter, his pretty little Cynthia. But Meyer was an expert, too, and he had confirmed the lump's presence. Deep inside, she was scared.

"I don't think it has to come out right now," Meyer said. "I'd like to watch it through one menstrual cycle. Perhaps it's a small cyst and it just may disappear after your next period, and that would save you an operation. Let's do the following. Let's watch the lump for the next ten days;

then I'll re-examine you and if it's still there, I'll remove it."

"Fine. In the meantime, I don't have to worry or do anything special?" she asked.

"One thing. I'm going to have my secretary arrange a xeromammogram for you."

She looked curiously at him.

"A mammogram is a special X ray of the breast. A xeromammogram is very similar. It uses a xeroxing process and paper rather than regular X-ray film."

She nodded. "I thought mammography was dangerous for young women."

"Only if you read too many magazines."

"I do." And she smiled.

"I wouldn't suggest routine mammography as a screening procedure in a young woman, but if you've got a lump, it's an important test, and yours will be done right here in the hospital with the lowest dose of X ray possible, less than a half rad per exposure. No risk. I guarantee it."

"Fine." She leaned back in her chair. She felt like changing the subject and talking to him. "You're an interesting man."

Meyer smiled. "Thank you."

"Besides being a nice person and a fine physician, you have nice eyes."

Meyer chuckled. "And you're a flirt."

He wasn't at all sure how to handle this situation. If he had met her anywhere else, he would have asked her out. He wouldn't have hesitated for a moment. Now, because she was a patient, it was ethically wrong. But he made up his mind: once the lump was removed, he was going to ask her out. She was exactly the kind of woman he wanted. There was nothing morally, ethically or medically wrong with his taking her out, *later*. They were two people, attracted to one another, and it was just that simple. There was no reason to set artificial limitations on the people to whom he could relate. So he was a doctor and she was a patient. So what? Obviously a doctor shouldn't routinely date his patients; he knew that. The doctor has an unfair advantage over them. But this time there would just have to be an exception. It wasn't a big thing. This was a benign breast biopsy, if that. Perhaps the lump would just disappear and she wouldn't even need a biopsy.

"I've always been a flirt," she chimed in on his thoughts. "Am I breaking the rules?"

"Sort of . . . there are just lots of rules in my life."

"You should be careful"—she smiled—"but every now and then you're going to have to side-step a rule or two, or you're never going to be happy."

Meyer was certain, now, their heads were in the same place. They'd been flirting with one another for the entire hour. "Have you ever been married?"

"No. Never even close," she said. "I don't know that I'll ever be married. I'm not even certain I want to be."

"Why do you say that?"

"I mean that I'm not sure that marriage is a good way to go. I'm not sure that we were meant to have one-on-one relationships that last forever." Why was she saying that? She had always wanted to marry. Every boy or man she'd ever been close to or dated, she'd fantasized about marrying. But it had never worked out for her. Maybe she'd wanted too much from them or maybe she didn't think she'd had enough to give or maybe she'd scared them all away by being too anxious. "I believe in relationships for as long as they last, a week, a month, a year, whatever. But when they're done, that's it. I leave."

"That's the way I do life, too," Meyer said.

"But I wouldn't run away from marriage," she added quickly. "If I met the right person, I mean. But there just aren't a lot of right people out there."

"For me either," Meyer said. "What are you doing to earn a living now?"

"Actually, I don't have to work. My father left me some money when he died. For a long while, I just wasted my time. Now I'm teaching dance therapy courses at the Neuropsychiatric Institute." She hesitated momentarily. "And I'm back in school. I dropped out of college when I was twenty and I'm back now, finishing, so I can get my master's."

Meyer smiled. He liked that kind of drive. "Do you like teaching?"

"I love it and I love the patients, especially the children. They're all very special to me."

"That's the way I feel about my students. Each one is very important to me. What are you getting your degree in?"

"Art."

The intercom buzzed and Meyer answered it. He hung up the phone and looked at Cynthia. She stared back into his dark brown eyes. "I'm way behind," he said.

She held out her hand as she got up. Meyer took it and walked her to the door.

"I'll see you soon," she said as she left, "and thank you."

Cynthia walked rapidly down the hospital corridor. She knew she was late and she looked for a public phone booth. A few heads turned to admire her as she passed. She'd become accustomed to the attention she attracted, but today she didn't bother to acknowledge it.

She found a phone booth, put a dime into the slot and dialed the club. "Could you page Alice Stern, please?" And she waited.

She thought about Jon Meyer: his tall lean body; his handsome bearded face; his confident voice. And then she thought about the lump.

"Alice, hi, Cynthia. I'm sorry I'm late, but I'm on my way. . . . Great . . . Thanks for waiting."

She hung up the phone and automatically found her way through the maze of hospital corridors and out to the parking lot. She didn't want to tell Alice about her check-up. She seldom shared anything of importance with any of the women at the club. There was already too much gossip and she didn't want a bunch of strangers ogling her and wondering what was wrong.

She sat in her car for a moment, staring out the window. She did feel relieved. Meyer had said it was nothing. But how long had the lump been there? Why now, why when everything was beginning to go so well? What had she done wrong to herself, or with her life?

"Nothing, I haven't done anything wrong!" she said out loud as she reached forward and started her car.

As she drove toward the club she imagined herself throwing a tennis ball into the air. She waited patiently for it to begin its downward fall and then she slammed it into Alice's forecourt. Then she felt a twinge of pain in her right breast. That was it. She had hurt herself playing tennis. She had banged the end of her racket into her breast or a ball had hit her there and its swelling had gone unnoticed. Or she had swung too hard, torn some blood vessels deep within the tissues of her breast and had created a small blood clot. She smiled, she had the answer.

She parked, changed and dashed out to the courts to meet Alice Stern.

6

The X-ray view box glared brightly in the dimly lit room as Dr. Heller began putting up the final set of films.

Susan Foster Heller was one of Jon Meyer's best friends. She was also the radiologist assigned to the surgical oncology service and she got to see Meyer every afternoon when his staff gathered in her small conference room for X-ray rounds prior to making walking rounds on the ward. During the thirty or forty minutes allotted, all the day's films, first of the inpatients and then of the outpatients, were reviewed.

There were only four films in the final set and they filled only three panes of the giant view box. Susan flipped off the unneeded lights as she presented the case.

"These xeromammograms were done this morning. They belong to a twenty-eight-year-old woman. The patient's mother had breast cancer and she died from it. There's no other family history of cancer. The patient has a one-centimeter mass in the upper outer quadrant of the right breast. It's deep and difficult to feel."

Cynthia's magnificent breasts had been reduced to four bluish images that almost completely filled the paper they were printed on. Mammograms were a high-class medical peep show: one-dimensional inner views of someone's breasts that allow the viewer to fantasize about the body connected to them.

Having had her mammograms taken earlier in the day, Cynthia was acutely aware of her body and, in particular, her breasts. She stood in front of the mirror in the large therapy room of the Neuropsychiatric Institute. As she straightened the sash on her leotards, she glanced quickly into the mirror re-examining her body's perfection. She flinched slightly at the thought of getting any heavier or of ever looking any different. Now the slight possibility of cancer, no matter how remote, sent chills through her.

Why had her body become so important to her? Since she was fifteen she'd had a good shape. But lately she'd begun to realize that maybe she'd been using her body in all the wrong ways, for the wrong purposes. Her thoughts were interrupted by the loud shuffling and the high-pitched giggles of her final class for the day.

Two of the youngsters, no more than seven or eight, came rushing into the room, racing up to her, demanding her immediate attention. She put her arms around them both, hugging them closely.

Helen, one of the psychiatric nurses, came over to her. "Hi, Cynthia. Can you make it through one more session today? The children are really looking forward to your class."

"I'm glad." And Cynthia headed for the phonograph next to the wall.

Some of the children sat down on the floor in the middle of the room while others wandered off toward some tables and chairs and sat down silently and alone in their own private worlds.

Helen came up to Cynthia and began whispering confidentially. "Arlene had a seizure yesterday so I'm going to stay in the observation room and keep an eye on her, just in case."

Cynthia looked up and smiled, nodding. "Thanks, Helen. I'm going to try something special today and I'm hoping it'll help Arlene."

Helen grimaced. "Go slowly, I really think she's ready to explode."

Cynthia let the needle down on the record and the music began to play softly. Then, without words, with just the music and her movements, Cynthia began to create a magical environment for the children. She was totally fluid as she began to sway back and forth. The children, fascinated, watched. Then she gestured to them to join her. One by one they stood up and started to sway with her. She gently herded them into a circle. Many of them joined hands as they continued to move around and then all of them joined hands.

Jessie, a small blond girl who hated to touch anything or anyone, didn't seem to notice that she was clutching someone's hand as she swayed back and forth to the music with her eyes closed.

Cynthia looked over at Helen to see if she had noticed the subtle breakthrough in Jessie's behavior. She had and she smiled.

Cynthia passed out crayons and paper and each of the children drew something. Then, one at a time, each child got up and, with Cynthia's help, danced out the colored patterns they had created.

Arlene had reluctantly drawn a picture filled with swirls and mountainlike humps all in blues and reds, but she'd remained in her isolated corner and refused to dance.

Cynthia turned from her and, with the drawing in her hand, began to swirl around in circles and then to leap as though she were scaling high mountains.

Arlene watched, transfixed, as Cynthia returned from her journey, from going around and around and up and down.

"I made it," Cynthia whispered breathlessly to Arlene. "What a trip."

"Can I come next time?" Arlene asked.

"The breasts are relatively dense," Dr. Heller continued, "and, although on physical exam we can feel the lump, we can't see it on these films. The architectural pattern is normal for a person of this age."

Susan pulled Cynthia's xeromammograms down and turned on the room lights. Meyer stood up. "X rays of the breast are not a substitute for a biopsy. If there's a suspicious lump in the breast that you can't see on X ray, you have to biopsy it; and if there's an abnormality shown on mammography that you can't feel, you've got to biopsy the abnormal area. The burden of proof is on the physician. In other words, you've got to treat the positive findings. With this patient, she's quite young and the mass feels benign. So I plan to watch it through one menstrual cycle. If it's still there, I'll biopsy it."

No discussion followed Meyer's totally routine comment.

As everyone began to leave for rounds, Meyer pulled Jerry Roberts aside. "That was your friend. I saw her a few days ago. It was a good pick-up on your part. A small lump in a big breast, most doctors would have missed it."

Jerry smiled. "I had a good teacher and it wasn't exactly unenjoyable work." When Meyer didn't smile back, Jerry was embarrassed and turned to leave. "Let me know what happens to her." And he headed for the ward.

Meyer went over to Susan and put his hand on her shoulder. "How's Louis?"

"Oh, he's fine, Jon. He always asks about you. When are you going to have dinner with us?"

"As soon as I finish with this grant application I've been working on. And by the way, you're due for another check-up."

Susan smiled back. She had a lovely round face with exceptionally expressive eyes. She was about five feet five inches tall, with shoulder-length straight brown hair. She was, perhaps, ten or fifteen pounds overweight, but still very attractive.

"Thanks for remembering. I'll be up this month."

"You promise?"

"I promise."

Meyer took the elevator up to 6-North. Looking at Cynthia Rogers' X rays had rekindled his thoughts about her. He had found his mind wandering and he was glad when rounds were finished.

He went back to his office, pulled her chart and dialed her number.

"Hello."
"Cynthia?"
"Yes."
"Hi, this is Dr. Meyer."
"Oh, hi."
"I've just seen your X rays and I didn't want you to worry. They're fine."
"Oh, good."
"They didn't show the lump, so we can't tell anything more about it."
"Then, they aren't fine?"
"Yes, they are," Meyer said. "They're absolutely normal for someone your age. They show none of the changes we associate with cancer."
"I'm glad."
"I knew you would be, and that's why I called as soon as I could."
"Well, thank you very much."
"You're welcome." There was a long pause. "I guess that's all," Meyer finally said.
"Well, thank you again. I really appreciate your calling."
"Okay, I'll see you next week. Let me know if it changes or there are any problems."
"I will."
Meyer said, "Good-bye," and he hung up. He would have liked to have seen her sooner. He opened the folder on his desk and began the evening's work.
Cynthia slowly put the receiver back in its cradle. It was nice of him to call, she thought. She wondered if he called all his patients right away. He wanted to tell her everything

was fine, that her xeromammograms were normal. But they didn't show the mass, so what good were they?

She slowly moved her left hand to her right breast and she began to feel. She probed deeply. Only the thin silk of her blouse covered her breast.

She pushed on the firm flesh as she changed the positions of her fingers. It was gone! She wanted to call back immediately, to tell Jon Meyer, but she had to make certain. She stood up, unbuttoned her blouse and removed it.

She walked into her bedroom, naked from the waist up, and sat down in front of her dressing mirror. She looked at herself. She knew people admired her body.

She began to probe her right breast again. Was it really gone? She kneaded the firm tissue between her fingertips and her ribs. She pressed deeply. She moved her right arm. Then she felt a hollow feeling deep within her as her fingers came upon the tiny mass. It was still there, unchanged. Of course, it was still there. She had only seen Meyer a few days ago, things like this took time. She felt chilled and a momentary wave of nausea spread through her. She took the rest of her clothes off and grabbed a long heavy robe from the closet. She put it on and went back into the living room. All of her hanging plants were dry and she began to water them. This was the first evening she had been home since her appointment with Jon Meyer.

She opened the curtains and then the glass sliding doors. She could hear the waves; occasionally she could see the breakers as they were caught by the moonlight. She watched them for a while. Their constant motion and their noise were usually soothing to her. Tonight they weren't.

She remembered the day she walked in and surprised her

mother. She remembered the long red slash across her chest and the bony ribs poking through where a warm soft breast used to be. But she didn't want to remember that image. It terrified her.

7

When Meyer saw Cynthia Rogers' name on his patient list for the afternoon, he got excited. He'd been looking forward to seeing her again.

As he stood in front of the examining room, his heart beat faster and he had the same wonderful momentary feeling of fear that he used to get before the whistle blew and he made his first move in a basketball game or that he got now, every time, just before he picked up the scalpel to open the abdomen at the beginning of a major operation.

He knocked, opened the door, walked in and looked at her face. She felt the same way he did. He knew it. He could tell by just looking at her eyes, by the way she looked at him. He stared for a moment, wrestled with the problem again and then made up his mind for the final time. If the lump was gone, he would ask her out. "Hi."

His fingers moved in ever-enlarging concentric circles as she lay on the examining table. "Don't be there," he said to himself as he probed deeply, knowing full well that this was just another part of his fantasy. He made his way slowly around the large circular area, carefully assessing the consistency of the substance he was feeling. Each time he moved his hand, her tissues bounced back to their original perfect contour. Finally, his fingers rolled over the small rubbery hard ball. The lump was unchanged and the disappointment he felt was personal and real. The necessary decision was obvious.

Cynthia dressed and went into Meyer's office. She'd felt the lump that morning and every morning for the past week and Meyer's findings were not a surprise to her.

"The lump is still there," he said. "Although we couldn't see it on X ray, I feel it ought to be removed."

Cynthia didn't really want to talk about an operation. "I've thought about you this last week . . . a lot," she said, deciding to tell him.

"I've thought about you, too."

"Medically?" she asked.

"Not only medically," Meyer answered.

The conversation was inappropriate from an ethical point of view, yet it didn't seem to matter. He had thought about her and she knew it. But he was her doctor and he had to talk to her as a doctor.

"Did you hear what I said about the lump?"

"Of course, I heard what you said."

"The lump has to be removed." He continued, "The odds are overwhelming that it's benign and there's no emergency. What I'm going to suggest to you is something a bit different from what's usually done. It's called 'the two-stage procedure.' First of all, most breast biopsies are done under general anesthesia, with the patient asleep. Your lump is small and deep, and it may be a little difficult, but I'd like to remove it using local anesthesia. You'd be in the operating room, but you'd be awake. Kind of like getting a tooth filled after the dentist gives you

Novocaine. . . . There's very little pain when the procedure is done under local and there are lots of advantages."

She closed her hands into fists.

"Most breast biopsies are done with the possibility of going ahead immediately and doing bigger surgery if cancer is found. In other words, everything is done in a single stage. When you go to sleep, you don't know whether you're going to wake up with a small Band-Aid over a biopsy or a large dressing over a mastectomy. I want to eliminate that worry. I'd like to schedule only a biopsy. Should the lump turn out to be something that requires more surgery, we can sit down together, discuss it in detail, order the additional tests that are necessary to make certain that the disease hasn't spread to other parts of the body; and then, a few days later, we can do, in a second stage, what needs to be done and what we've both agreed on doing."

Her eyes widened as what he was saying sank in. "I thought you said the lump was nothing."

"I did. But there's no way to be one hundred per cent certain until it's been removed and looked at through a microscope by the pathologist. That's why we're doing the biopsy in the first place. I'd be doing you an injustice if I didn't remove it. There is a very small possibility that this lump is malignant."

"You mean cancer?"

"Yes," he said. "It's a possibility, but an extremely unlikely one."

She leaned forward. "How unlikely?" She wanted to hear it again.

"Tremendously unlikely. So unlikely that you shouldn't

worry about it. The lump doesn't feel like cancer and the X rays of your breast are absolutely normal.

"I'd like to do the biopsy with a minimum of disruption to your personal life . . . with you as an outpatient. You won't eat or drink anything after midnight on the night before surgery. That night you'll take a sleeping pill. The next morning, one of your friends can bring you to the hospital. You'll be premedicated, I'll do the biopsy and you'll go home later in the day."

"What you're saying is that no matter what the lump turns out to be, I'll go home a few hours after the biopsy."

"Exactly. We won't even know the diagnosis that day. It takes the pathologist twenty-four hours to make permanent sections and study the slides. But it's much better that way, because then he's not rushed."

She leaned back and looked carefully at him. "Why should I be awake for the biopsy?"

"It's simpler and safer," Meyer answered. "It can be dangerous to get general anesthesia."

"How dangerous?"

"Well, for your age group, not very. But it's still more risky than having the procedure under local."

"And it won't hurt if it's done under local?"

"You'll know I'm working. You'll feel some pulling. But most women are delighted when I do it this way."

She nodded. "All right." She wanted to show him that she could take it, that she was brave. "But what happens if I decide against local anesthesia and I want to go to sleep? I don't think I will, but I just want to know."

"It's important that you know. It's your right so that you can give what we call 'informed consent.' If you decide to have general anesthesia, you'll be admitted to the hospital overnight, have the biopsy and if anything more has to be done it can all be done either at the same time or a few days later. It's up to you."

"In all honesty," she said—her palms were wet—"if I needed to have something more than a biopsy, I almost think I'd prefer to have it all at one sitting. The thought of waiting around for days, knowing that I had to have my breast removed, would be very difficult for me."

"I'd help you," Meyer said. "But the chances that you have cancer are so small and biopsy under local makes so much sense."

Maybe she wasn't as enthusiastic about the two-stage procedure as he was, but over the years he'd found that one step at a time gave women a chance to think, to talk to their families and to work out their lives before a major operation took place.

It seemed so important to him. She smiled weakly. "Let me think about it for a little while."

"Okay. But if you decide to have the whole thing at one time, then you have to decide before surgery which operation you're going to have, in case the lump is cancer."

He got up from his desk. For a moment Cynthia hoped that he'd come over to her and just hold her. But instead he went over to a shelf and pulled out a folder.

"Let me show you some pictures and I think it'll make the whole thing clearer."

He pulled a series of artist's drawings from the folder and laid them out on the desk. This was too bad, he thought. If she would agree to the two-stage procedure, he wouldn't have to go through this now. If by some chance the lump was malignant, there would be ample time to discuss procedures and they would have far more meaning to her. By discussing it now, it was all too hypothetical, a needless and painful exercise.

"This is a normal woman. Her breasts are about equal in size." Cynthia nodded.

He pointed to the second picture. "Now, this is the same woman, but part of her left breast has been removed. You can see that the left breast is smaller than the right. This is called a 'partial mastectomy.' It's an experimental procedure. We're not sure how good it's going to be."

"It doesn't *look* bad," she said.

"No, it doesn't. That's its real advantage. Cosmetically, it's the best procedure. But you may be leaving cancer behind when you do it."

"The next drawing shows the left breast completely removed. However, the muscles behind the breast have been left in place. This is what a 'total' or 'simple' mastectomy looks like. Only the breast has been removed.

"A 'modified radical mastectomy' removes the whole breast and the lymph glands and fat in the armpit. And it looks exactly the same as the 'total mastectomy.' However, it's a more complete operation.

"This final picture shows the same woman having undergone a standard 'radical mastectomy.' That's the procedure that's been done for the last eighty years. It removes the whole breast, the pectoral muscles behind the breast and the fat and lymph nodes in the armpit."

"These two are awful," Cynthia said, pointing to the last two drawings in which the entire breast had been removed.

Actually the drawings were pretty good, Meyer thought.

They really didn't do justice to the operations. The real thing looked worse. "If you have cancer, it has to be treated."

"Which one of these operations is best?"

"I would say that for most patients the standard radical or the modified radical offer the best statistical chance of cure. If you take only part of the breast, I think you're increasing the risk. I'd be willing to do a partial mastectomy only under certain circumstances."

"Would you do that for me, if I wanted it?"

"I wouldn't recommend it; but if you wanted it, I'd do it. It depends on so many factors—size of the lump, location of the lump, size of the breast, age of the patient . . . the psychological overlay. Some women have told me that they'd rather die than lose a breast. If that were the case, then of course, I'd do a partial mastectomy."

"My breasts are very important to me," Cynthia said. "They're the best part of my body."

"Your whole body is lovely," he blurted out.

"Thank you." And she finally relaxed and gave him a real smile.

What the hell was he doing? he thought to himself. Why didn't he just pick up the phone and send her to one of his colleagues? It would be so much simpler.

Beneath her smile, Cynthia was worried. The idea of an operation was beginning to overwhelm her. Both her parents were dead. She didn't like to involve any of the people she worked with in her personal life and there was nobody at the club she felt she could share this problem with. She really had no one. She had isolated herself and she was alone. . . . She looked warmly at Meyer. Then she held out her hand. "Can I make you dinner tonight?"

He had never dated a patient in his life, let alone one that he was about to operate on. He knew it was wrong. But he was normal and human and he wanted her. It was just that simple and he gave up struggling over an answer. He just couldn't say no.

He took her hand. "I'd love to have dinner with you."

After she'd left, Meyer realized that she hadn't made a final decision and he called his secretary.

"Betty, book Miss Rogers for a right-breast biopsy under general anesthesia and a possible modified radical mastectomy if malignant."

And it was done. He booked the case that way so that Cynthia would have total freedom of choice. It was much simpler to back down to a smaller operation or only a biopsy under local than to go the other way. He purposely scheduled the case for a week from Thursday so there would be plenty of time to talk about it.

As Meyer drove toward Cynthia's apartment he was filled with excitement and anticipation. In terms of what he thought was beautiful, Cynthia Rogers was the most physically perfect woman that he had ever seen. From the very beginning there had been something special about her: the way she carried herself; her self-confidence; her openness; her drive. But it was more than that. There was an animal attraction between them, so strong that Meyer was about to break a rule that he'd never even considered breaking before, dating a patient.

After they'd first met, he'd thought the problem through

a dozen times. Today, when he saw her again, he finally decided: he would ask her out, but only if the lump was gone; otherwise, he would wait until he'd finished taking care of her. But when she'd asked him out, she'd taken him by surprise and, automatically, he'd said yes.

Meyer routinely made decisions quickly, but unlike his surgical decisions, he often agonized over his personal ones. At first he was very uncomfortable, and after she'd left his office he'd felt anxious about his decision. But now that he was on his way, he was glad and he was determined not to feel guilty.

So what if she was a patient? She had all the potential for being the right person. He had to make an exception and he fantasized the perfect relationship, the one that had eluded him for thirty-eight years.

As he turned onto the Pacific Coast Highway, he thought about Nancy. There was a woman with potential. She was lovely and intelligent and she was a doctor, his equal. What more could he have wanted? He'd respected her from the day they'd met. And yet, their marriage had been a failure. There had always been something missing. There was no spark, ever, not even in the beginning. They'd been like brother and sister. He wasn't even sure why he'd married her. He just had. "We looked good together on paper," he'd always said.

But Cynthia seemed to have that intangible component, that missing spark. His thoughts shifted and he found himself thinking about Cynthia, comparing her with Nancy, trying to make decisions about the kind of relationship they were going to have. He wondered why he was getting so far ahead of himself with someone he hardly knew.

Cynthia looked into the mirror a final time, brushed her hair back away from her face and then answered the door.

"Hi, Jon." She liked calling him by his first name.

Her long, thick, blond hair hung down loosely and reached below her shoulders. She wore tight white silk pants with a matching top. Nothing was exposed, but you could see every part of her body. When she moved she was muscular and fluid. She was curvaceous, but there was no fat. She was totally appealing to Meyer, healthy and fresh-looking.

"You look lovely." And he handed her a 1961 bottle of Château Batailley. It was a much better wine than he would ordinarily have brought on a first date.

She took the wine and smiled, said, "Thank you" and looked him over. "No ties allowed at this restaurant."

Meyer grinned as he took off his jacket and began complying with her order by loosening his tie. "I'm sorry for the suit. I haven't been home today."

She squinted playfully. "I thought it looked familiar."

He slipped the tie off from around his neck. "Clean shirt, though. I keep a supply in my office for emergencies."

"I'm happy to be considered an emergency." She extended her hand and led him into the living room.

Much of the west wall was glass and both sliding doors were open, allowing the fresh cold air and the smell of the ocean to drift into the room. There were perhaps thirty plants hanging from the ceiling and placed about the room. The shelves along one wall were filled with books and art objects. Everything seemed to have a place and there was no clutter.

They sat down on the small couch in front of the fireplace. Cynthia took a bottle of white wine out of the ice bucket on the coffee table and she poured two glasses. As she handed Meyer a glass, he twisted around in his corner of the couch so he could face her.

"Now, you can tell me all about yourself. Did you always want to be a doctor?"

Meyer wanted to toast something, but he wasn't certain what: to Cynthia, to the beginning of a relationship, to something. But it all sounded trite.

"Always," he answered. "Since I was little."

"Why?"

There were so many reasons. He didn't even know where to begin. He didn't even know the right reason. When he was fourteen he'd grown very close to a sick old lady on his paper route. He used to mow her lawn and do odd jobs for her. She'd grown very fond of him and to please her he'd promised that he'd study medicine, someday. Although he wasn't at all certain if he would. When he'd met her physician, the old man had discouraged him. "What do you want to be a doctor for, people cough on you and you have to get up in the middle of the night?"

But it really went back even further than that. When he was little, he'd been afraid to die, afraid of forever. And doctors were like God: they dealt with life and death; they had power and they cured diseases. That's what Jon Meyer wanted to have and to do.

He was also poor when he was young and doctors were rich. But that wasn't the answer. Meyer was never going to become wealthy working at the university.

He smiled at her. "I don't have a good answer right now."

"What made you choose surgery, then?" She slipped her shoes off and put her feet on the table in front of the fire.

He looked at her. She even had pretty feet.

"Just warming my toes," and she smiled.

Meyer thought back to when he'd begun his surgical residency. He'd taken call every other night for five years. It had been hard and constant work, always with new problems to solve. Yet, those had been the best years of his life.

"You have to be arrogant, aggressive and ruthless to be a surgeon; and I'm all of those."

Cynthia shook her head. "I don't think so. I wouldn't invite someone like that to my apartment. You're sensitive and you're thoughtful."

Meyer smiled. "How could you ask your doctor for a date? How could you ask someone who'd just examined you, who's going to operate on you?"

"How could you accept?" She looked straight at him.

Meyer didn't answer.

"Got you," she said. "How could I?" she asked rhetorically. "It was easy. I asked and you said yes. You want something, you have to go out and get it. My father taught me that and he was right."

"Do you want me?" Meyer asked.

"I don't know. I want an answer to my question—why'd you become a surgeon?"

Meyer laughed. He liked her confidence. He sat back and thought for a moment.

"Actually it was a relatively late decision in my medical career. All through medical school I wanted to be an internist, a diagnostician. I felt surgery was too technical, no thinking. You took a bunch of things out of the belly, hooked what was left back together and hoped that it all worked. It's funny, because when I was a kid I liked to do things with my hands, build airplanes, ferris wheels with Erector sets. Anyway, everybody in medical school who was creative with their hands wanted to be a surgeon, except me. But during the beginning of my senior year I was on the surgical service and something happened that changed my life. I got a chance to do something.

"One day the chief resident said, 'Meyer, tomorrow, when we go to the operating room, you'll be the surgeon on the last case, rather than the assistant.'

"The next day, Jon Meyer, the great diagnostician, would lower himself to the mundane chore of removing a lump from beneath the skin of some unsuspecting victim. What a waste of time, I thought, but the truth was . . . I was scared shitless. I couldn't even sleep that night."

Cynthia laughed.

"My heart pounded when I scrubbed in the next day. I snuck into the operating room, hoping no one would know I was there.

"We draped the patient's entire body with green sheets. It was ludicrous. All he had was a mass about this big," and Meyer held up his thumb and forefinger with about half an inch of space between them. He stopped for a moment, realizing that Cynthia had a similar problem. She smiled at him, reassuring him not to worry, that he hadn't upset her, but her heart began to beat faster.

"Go on," she said as she continued to hold her smile.

"Anyway, I put some Novocaine into the skin and all of a sudden the nurse banged the scalpel into my hand without my having to ask for it and my hand began to shake. I was afraid.

"'Relax,' the chief resident barked. He wasn't very patient with me. 'This is nothing. Make an incision right here, about a half inch long.' He made a mark on the skin with the instrument he was holding. I was supposed to cut on the dotted line like I was cutting out an airplane from the back of a cereal box. I drew the knife blade over the line and made an incision about one millionth of an inch deep. So superficial it didn't even bleed.

"'Meyer,' he said sarcastically to me, 'you've got to cut through the skin.'

"I tried again and I failed, but the third time"—Meyer grinned—"the patient bled and I became a surgeon. The lump turned out to be a sebaceous cyst, sort of a fancy pimple."

Cynthia laughed. "I like happy endings."

Meyer smiled. "When I walked out of the operating room, I felt good and I hadn't expected it. I'd removed the disease and I had actually cured somebody. I felt fantastic. And right then and there, I decided to become a surgeon. But then I got scared. What if I couldn't do it? What if all the knots I tied fell apart? So I went to see the chief of surgery, who, like all chiefs of surgery was a son-of-a-bitch. I told him about my insecurities, about my quick decision and so on. He looked at me menacingly over his half glasses.

"'Meyer,' he said, 'can you tie your shoelaces?'

"'Yes, sir,' I replied.

"'Good. Then you can become a surgeon. Now, get the hell out of my office!' And that was it."

Cynthia laughed again. "So I'm just another victim."

She moved closer to him and he put his arm around her. The shadows made by the fire and the candles were changing rhythmically over her. Meyer leaned over and kissed her softly on the lips and she kissed him back.

They talked for two hours about everything, about themselves, about their pasts and about their goals.

Cynthia finally took him by the hand and led him into the small dining room. The table was set with flowers and candles. They picked at their salads and they looked at one another. She reached her hand across the table and he took it. He held it and stroked it, then she gently slipped it away. She brought the main course in and they picked at that and sipped the red wine he'd brought. They weren't very hungry.

Had she set them up? She wondered. This really wasn't like her. There was no way out for either of them, not tonight, anyway. It was too perfect an evening. She'd made the whole apartment warm and inviting, virtually a cavern of candles and good smells. She hoped he realized that he was special, that she was making an exception for him, that she didn't even date that much anymore.

He looked at her face, her perfect skin, and he wanted to kiss her. He got up, walked around the table and gently kissed her on the lips. She stood up, put her arms around him and kissed him back, at first softly, then with increasing passion. She laid her head on his chest and they just held one another and then he kissed her again.

He was intoxicated by her smell, her movements, her body, by her presence. He took her hand and led her back into the living room and they made love in front of the fireplace. Afterward, they touched, held hands, kissed and talked until one in the morning.

Meyer made it a policy not to go out the night before major surgery. He always felt obliged to be home early and well rested before he operated. He liked to spend the evening thinking entire cases through, analyzing all the possibilities. What could go wrong and how he would handle it if something happened. It was war: Meyer and the patient and whoever else wanted to help, all of them against cancer. In spite of this ritualistic preparation though, he often lost.

But Meyer didn't have to operate in the morning and he wondered if a case had been scheduled whether he would have come anyway.

Then he thought about whether or not he should sleep over. He seldom slept anywhere except in his own house or occasionally at the hospital. Basically, he was selfish. He wanted a good night's sleep and most of his women friends were willing to comply with his needs. As far as tomorrow was concerned, he had teaching rounds at 7:00 in the morning and his clothes for the next day were at his house. . . . Anyway, who could sleep on a small bed with another person?

When Cynthia finally asked him, he took her in his arms.

"Of course I'm going to stay. Where the hell did you think I was going to sleep?"

They touched all night and they didn't sleep well, but it was wonderful being close to someone that he wanted to be close to. Every time he awoke, he made certain that she was there. And every time he made certain, he got excited.

They made love again at 5:30, and by 6:00 he'd left.

He drove home, showered, dressed and made it to 6-North by 6:55. He was always punctual.

8

Cynthia turned over restlessly. She was wide awake now, staring at the ceiling.

It had been a beautiful evening. She pulled Jon's pillow close to her body, burying her face in his scent. She inhaled deeply, smelling him, wishing he could have stayed a little longer.

She probably should have jumped up and made him a good breakfast before he'd left. But by the time they'd finished making love and talking, he'd gotten dressed quickly and gone. But she wished she had thought to offer.

And she wondered about last evening—had she done the right thing, said the right words? Did he really like her as much as he seemed to?

In the past, she'd seized opportunities to become quickly and totally involved with other men, but Jon Meyer was clearly different. He was what she wanted! She smiled, recreating the images of them together: eating, talking, laughing . . . loving. She replayed conversations in her mind, the ones they'd had and the ones she wished they would have. She tried to imagine herself the way she would look and be the next time he saw her.

Suddenly she frowned. Here she was doing it again: putting all the pressures of perfection on a relationship that hadn't even had time to develop, that really didn't even exist, yet.

What if there was no next time? What if he didn't call? Suddenly she felt empty and alone. She tried to shake it off—it was stupid and groundless. Almost unconsciously, she pushed her hand under the pillow and began to probe her right breast.

The fear that overcame her whenever she reaffirmed the lump's presence returned, compounding her concerns about Jon and their future. She pulled the covers tightly around her neck and rolled over onto her stomach.

"It's benign," she thought. And it had brought them together, hadn't it? She tried to go back to sleep.

Meyer walked briskly down the corridor, almost bouncing along, fueled by some secret source of energy. He joined a group of students and residents, and they started off.

Rounds followed a predictable pattern: always beginning at the 6-North nursing station and proceeding methodically, in the same direction, from room to room, down and back the A, B and C corridors, to the surgical intensive care unit, then downstairs to the recovery room.

In the multibedded areas, they always started with the bed closest to the door and moved clockwise, visiting and examining every patient and answering their questions.

But most of the time on rounds was spent outside the rooms, in the halls. By discussing each case in the corridor, Meyer tried to prevent the often overly sensitive cancer patient from overhearing, from misinterpreting words or being alarmed by any of the questions asked or comments made.

New patients' histories were presented in great detail, along with plans for their management and any possible alternatives in treatment. Patients who had been previously discussed were summarized and their progress reported. What happened after each patient was presented depended on many factors: the quality of the presentation; the knowledge and poise of the student or resident presenting; the depth with which the disease being presented had previously been discussed by the current resident or student group; and Meyer's mood, which today seemed especially jovial.

Meyer loved firing question after question at students and residents, taking them as far as they could go and then often one step further, but always as part of a learning game. Whenever Meyer backed anyone into an intellectual corner, he usually helped him out.

The first patient was Mr. Michael Baum, a sixty-two-year-old frail Jewish man. During the past week his jaundiced skin had been the subject of two or three long discussions in the hall outside his room, and in X-ray conference. Now the small army in white gathered around his bed while Meyer pushed gently down on Baum's abdomen. Baum stared intently at Meyer; the whites of his eyes were very yellow.

"It's all set for tomorrow," Meyer said gently.

Mr. Baum nodded. He was relieved. One way or another in the morning there would finally be an answer to what was causing his condition.

"What time, please?" he asked with a thick Jewish accent. "I want to tell my wife."

"First thing in the morning," Meyer said. "They'll pick you up about six-thirty, maybe a quarter to seven."

Mr. Baum continued to nod. "Thank you for everything." He looked around at all the young faces, many of whom had and would continue to play a role in his care. "Thank you, all."

Meyer smiled and pulled the covers back. "Dr. Foley and I will be back this afternoon and we can go over any of your final questions about the operation."

"What time? I want my wife to be here."

"Two," Meyer answered. As the group moved back into the hall, Meyer was the last to leave, remaining behind to give Mr. Baum a few supportive words.

The group formed a small circle outside the next room. Referring back to Mr. Baum, Meyer made some comments about obstructive jaundice, the operative approach they would use and the generally dismal prognosis for cancer of the pancreas.

Then he asked who had the next patient.

Ann Collins smiled, taking her cue from Meyer, and began:

"Mary Alvarez is a forty-two-year-old Mexican-American lady. About five months ago she noticed a small mass in her left breast. She did nothing about it, but became alarmed recently when it increased in size. We saw her last week in the clinic and did an outpatient needle biopsy under local. When that came back malignant, we got her in and did a complete metastatic work-up. All of her blood and urine tests were normal, as well as her chest X ray, bone and liver scans. Dr. Roberts, with Dr. Meyer's help, did a left modified radical mastectomy five days ago. The drainage tubes were removed yesterday. She's up, eating and, in general, doing well. She has no limitation of her arm movements and could probably go home tomorrow."

Meyer smiled. He liked the compact, thorough and professional way that Ann presented her cases. "Tell us about her estrogen binding test and what it means."

"Well," Ann said as she turned toward the other students, "that's a new test, but it's very important. We took a little piece of the tumor and sent it to the lab for a determination as to whether it had receptor sites for estradiol, and it did."

"And what does that mean?"

"It means that Mrs. Alvarez' tumor is hormonally dependent. So if it ever recurs, some form of hormone manipulation should be the first treatment."

Meyer nodded and added, "Every patient with new or recurrent breast cancer should have this test, if possible. What about her lymph nodes?" he asked.

Ann nodded negatively. "The original biopsy was infiltrating ductal cancer, but I don't know the status of the final report. I haven't seen it yet."

"I have," Jerry Roberts chimed in. "I reviewed the slides with the pathologist yesterday afternoon. All her nodes were negative . . . all thirty-one of them." And he smiled.

So, Meyer thought to himself—two things had happened that were worth smiling about. First of all, all negative lymph nodes meant a much better prognosis for Mrs. Alvarez. Second, Jerry Roberts had just shined. It's called roundsmanship: knowing something that no one else knows; being able to cite some strange piece of medical literature; or making certain to see the pathology report before anyone else does.

Meyer wasn't certain which turned Jerry on more. Ordinarily, he would have let it pass, perhaps even been proud of him, but today Jerry's attitude bothered him. He looked carefully at Jerry, who dropped his smile. "Ann is the student assigned to this case. You really should have told her about the report."

Then he turned to Ben Silverman, the psychiatric resident on the service. "Medically, Mrs. Alvarez is in good shape. Let's talk about another aspect of this case. Ben, what can you tell us about her? What made her wait five months before seeing a doctor?"

When Meyer had first arrived at the university, one of the earliest negotiations he had entered into was with the chief of the Department of Psychiatry. Together, they established a rotation for psychiatric residents on the surgical oncology service. The residents' job was to probe deeply into the emotional problems of cancer patients and help the patients, their families and the surgical team deal effectively with them.

Every week the service had an in-depth conference about one patient and his or her family. They explored the feelings caused by cancer and what they as physicians could do about them.

They also had a weekly group therapy session led by the psychiatric resident in which they talked not about individual patients but rather about the difficulty of treating cancer victims and how they as doctors and people were being affected emotionally by their close proximity to these patients.

It had never been Meyer's plan to make surgical residents into psychiatrists, but Meyer wanted his residents to learn to relate to people, not just to diseases. Clearly, Meyer's students were learning this earlier in their careers than he had in his.

"Well, Dr. Meyer," Ben said, "Mrs. Alvarez has been married for about twenty years, loves her husband. She has four kids and she's always worked hard to help support the family.

"When she found the lump, she wasn't terribly concerned. She didn't think much of it. She never heard of breast self-examination. She never heard of mammography and, at first, she didn't think of cancer.

"After three months, it finally dawned on her that something might be wrong. But then she waited another two months. She rationalized the delay, saying that she couldn't afford to take the day off from work. If she did take the day off, she had no medical insurance and she wouldn't be able to pay the doctor bills. Actually, these excuses were all secondary.

"When she first realized that there was a problem, that she might have cancer, that she might lose a breast, she got terribly frightened. She comes from a Mexican-American macho culture where the women are extremely supportive of their men. She wasn't sure how her husband would react if she lost a breast. She was one scared, uninformed lady and that was the primary problem."

"Not an uncommon story," Meyer added. "What are you doing to help her?"

"Well," Ben answered, "as soon as we knew that she had cancer and would require a mastectomy, we started her in counseling. We're doing some of it with her husband during the evenings so that he doesn't have to lose any time from work. We've already had a Spanish-speaking volunteer from the American Cancer Society's Reach to Recovery Program speak with her. They've had a couple of meetings and the volunteer has been able to answer her questions in a way that no one else could have."

Meyer smiled. "That all sounds great. Let's go see her."

Rounds finished at 9:30. As Meyer turned to go down the corridor, Ann Collins stepped up in front of him, blocking his path.

"Thanks for sticking up for me."

"Jerry should have told you about the status of Mrs. Alvarez' nodes." And then Meyer smiled. "Or you should have beaten him to the pathology report."

"Is that what surgery's all about?" she asked, seriously.

"No," Meyer answered. "That's not what it's about at all."

"I want to talk with you about something. Do you have time?"

Meyer looked at his watch. He wanted to get to his office. He'd been thinking about Cynthia between patients and that was unusual for him because he seldom thought about the women in his life while he was working, especially during teaching rounds.

"Sure, if you don't mind walking me down to my office."

They both took off down the corridor.

"You know my elective with you is over this week."
Meyer nodded. "Yes."

"I'm on general surgery next month . . . on Dr. Stoner's service. And I've been warned. I hear he's tough on women, particularly those who want to become surgeons."

Meyer smiled. "You'll be all right. You handled me, didn't you?"

"But you're nice to everyone." She laughed.

"I don't think you'll have any problem."

"Well, it's a small service, just one resident and me."

"You'll just have to be as good a student as you can be, and smile at him once in a while."

Meyer put his hand on Ann's shoulder. "Look, it's harder for a woman, that's true. But Stoner is good practice. Use him as an opportunity to learn how to deal with this problem when you get out there in the real world. And he's a hell of a good surgeon."

"Okay, thanks. I may be back to cry on your shoulder." Ann smiled at him as she turned and left.

Meyer went into his office, sat down at his desk, looked at the phone, picked it up and dialed Cynthia's number.

"What's gotten into you?" Alice Stern asked.

"Nothing," Cynthia answered. She took a sip of her iced tea.

Alice smiled. "Cynthia, darling, you can't fool me. I've known you too long. I can sense something. You played a couple of the best sets of tennis I've ever seen you play." Waiting for an answer, Alice's smile broadened, her white teeth contrasting with her deeply tanned artificially tight-skinned face.

"I met a nice man."

"I knew it! I knew it! Tell me about him."

"Not yet. We've only been out once."

Alice was a small wiry woman and she patted her tiny chest in protest. "You can tell me."

"There's nothing to tell." She paused, but Alice didn't respond, forcing Cynthia to continue. "He's a doctor . . . we're going out again tonight."

"I know every doctor in town. . . . Come on, who is he?"

Cynthia pursed her lips and nodded, no. "When I'm ready. Okay?" Cynthia liked Alice. Alice had been something of a surrogate mother to her after Cynthia's father had died, but it had always tended to be on a rather superficial level. And Alice was a club member with a big mouth.

Before Alice had a chance to pry any further, Emma Hoffman, a plump young girl in her early twenties, came over to the table. Avoiding Alice's gaze, she ducked her head under the sun umbrella and spoke directly to Cynthia.

"Excuse me, Cynthia," Emma began shyly, "but do you think you'll have some time today?"

Cynthia looked at her watch and nodded. "From one until a quarter to two, then I have to go to work. Okay?" She smiled up at Emma.

"Oh, thanks, Cynthia. I've got court seven." And she turned and sidled off toward the ladies' locker rooms.

"Why do you insist on playing with her?" Alice asked. "She'll ruin your game."

"No, she won't. And I play with her because she asks me to."

It was almost 4:30 and Meyer was staring at the blank yellow legal pad lying on his desk. He hadn't written a word since he'd sat down almost thirty minutes ago to revise his grant proposal.

As the day had gone on, Cynthia seemed to be occupying a progressively greater proportion of his thoughts. It bothered him, yet it thrilled him. Almost like a child with a new toy, he couldn't wait for the day to be over, to get home and to be with her again.

He sat back, finally accepting that he would get nothing further done. He put his feet up on the corner of his desk, sipped his coffee and thought about last evening, how much he'd enjoyed her company, the perfection of her body. Their minds and bodies had gone together as though they'd been friends and lovers for a long time. He thought about how he'd first met her, how he'd looked up into her face from across this desk. Then he finally realized that what he was doing was absolutely crazy. Cynthia Rogers was a patient. He was a surgeon . . . her surgeon. She was booked for surgery in eight days and he'd been in bed with her, making love.

There was no question about it—if the chairman of the Department of Surgery or the dean of the medical school, or for that matter if *anyone* found out about it, they wouldn't like it. It was poor judgment. It was in poor taste. It was totally and obviously inappropriate!

He picked up the phone and pressed the intercom button. "Betty, get me Ted Stoner, please."

There was only one solution. He'd get someone else to do the case and that would be that. It was a benign lump and it didn't make a goddamn bit of difference who removed it.

Stoner was a technically superb surgeon who, like himself, did breast biopsies through circumareolar incisions, incisions that were virtually invisible after they'd healed. Meyer had no qualms about letting him operate on Cynthia.

As soon as he'd made the decision, he felt better. He watched the phone. When the intercom light went on, but before Betty could buzz him, he picked up the receiver. "Yes."

"Dr. Stoner is away until Monday."

"Thanks, Betty." He thought for a second. "Listen, have his secretary block out an hour next Thursday morning. I want him to biopsy one of the patients I saw yesterday . . . Miss Rogers. Tell her that I'll okay it with him on Monday."

Meyer hung up and made a note on his calendar. He felt much better.

He grabbed a hamburger and ate it during X-ray rounds. He made ward rounds with the residents, got back to his office by 6:45, answered a few phone calls and left the hospital. He was tired, but excited.

The traffic seemed unusually light and Meyer found himself unconsciously breaking the speed limit most of the way home. He got off the freeway at Sunset Boulevard and wound his way up into the hills on roads that seemed to have been created for his Porsche.

Cynthia's yellow Morgan was in his driveway. She'd pulled it way over to the right and Meyer had no problem slipping his car in next to it. The two cars looked good together, he thought.

He was surprised when she opened the front door and came out of his house to greet him.

"How'd you get in?"

She came up to him and kissed him gently on the lips. "First things first."

He pulled her closer and felt the warmth of her body. He was immediately comfortable with her as she welcomed him to his own home.

"I sat on the front steps for a few minutes and then I decided to break in. It was easy, the back door was open."

Meyer smiled. "What if I'd had a big dog?"

"I'd have given him your steak dinner and he would have fallen madly in love with me."

Meyer put his arm around her waist and they walked through the hallway into the living room. There was a log smoldering in the fireplace.

She smiled coquettishly at him. "I'm good at starting fires only when there's a jet of natural gas under the logs."

Meyer laughed and sat down on the slate ledge surrounding the elevated fireplace. He crumpled up some newspaper, shoved in a few kindling sticks and lit it.

In one corner of the room there was a wooden chess table separating two soft green easy chairs. A stuffed gorilla contemplating his next move sat on one of the green chairs. He was large enough so that if you looked at him quickly, particularly in the middle of the night, he seemed quite real. On a chrome and glass *étagère* there was a hippopotamus collection: wooden, stone, glass, leather, ceramic, all kinds.

"What's this thing you've got for hippos?" Cynthia asked.

"Someone gave me one once. Then I bought one. Then all of a sudden, I was a collector. Now, everyone gives me hippos. It's almost gotten out of hand."

"When is your birthday?" she asked, with a smile.

There were a dozen other creatures scattered about the room.

"You must love animals. Which one of these dead things is your favorite?"

"This buffalo." He picked up the piece from the glass coffee table in front of the fireplace. "I got it in Colorado, in 1962, in a little Indian shop. It's hand-carved from clay and fired, but it looks almost like wood." He handed it to Cynthia and she admired its detail and weight.

"Beautiful."

"It's the first animal I ever bought, and the only piece I took with me when I got divorced. Look how big his chest is, how virile he is."

"Is that why you like him?"

"That's one reason. He's just beautifully made. I like things that are technically perfect."

Cynthia put the buffalo down and walked over to the sliding glass doors. She unlocked one of them and pushed it back.

"Why did you get divorced?" She'd been wondering why a man of Jon's age and stature didn't have a nice cozy home with a wife and children scurrying around in it.

"I'd better get a bottle of wine before I start on that."

As Meyer disappeared, Cynthia stepped outside onto the redwood decking of a small, very private pool. It was a perfect evening, a warm balmy summer breeze coming in off the ocean. She looked out at the expanse of the city lights below as she sat down in a chair next to the round wooden table.

Meyer joined her with an open bottle of red wine and two glasses.

"It didn't work out."

"What does that mean?"

"Oh, I guess when I got married, I just didn't want to be married. I was used to living by myself, doing whatever I wanted, whenever I wanted. I was totally selfish and I didn't want a relationship."

"Why did you get married then?" . . . And what's different about you now? she wondered.

"Nancy was a fabulous woman and she was persistent. Somehow she convinced me that if I let her go, there was no hope for me. I knew the day I got married that it wouldn't work out, but I did it anyway. I was a resident at the time. I was seldom home. I was routinely unfaithful. Yet, I thought I loved her. To this day I care for her. I want her to be happy. I want her life to be good."

"Did she ever remarry?"

"Right away . . . within a year. She married a psychiatrist—they're much easier to live with than surgeons. They listen to you. I guess it was never really a marriage. I just didn't want an all-consuming commitment to one person."

Cynthia wondered if he ever wanted to make that commitment, but she couldn't bring herself to ask. "The view is spectacular," she said.

"I loved this house the minute I saw it," Meyer said. "It's completely private with a view of the world. Do you see those tall lights?" And he pointed out to the right.

"Yes."

"That's Century City."

"This enormous city . . . it makes me feel so small and unimportant . . . like I haven't done anything at all with my life."

"You shouldn't feel that way. Think of those kids you teach. What would they do without you? There aren't many people who could or would do it. You're making a real contribution." He leaned over and kissed her. "Where do you play tennis?"

Cynthia laughed. So *that* was what he wanted to know about her! He laughed too, realizing that was the last thing he really cared about.

"At the Holmby Hills Country Club."

"How'd you become a member there?"

"My father left it to me when he died. It's about the only place I remember having any real time with him, and I like tennis."

"Didn't your father spend much time with you?"

"Not really. He was a big busy businessman and, after my mother died, I think his work was all he really cared about. But he used to take me to the club on Sundays and play tennis with me, or watch me in a match. He liked to see me win. Winning was important to him whether it was on a tennis court or in a board room."

"Did he ever remarry?"

"No, never. He always said mother was special. And she was. She was terribly beautiful and so kind to everyone. She was a very generous woman, not only with things, but with her time and her energy." Tears came to Cynthia's eyes as she remembered. She thought about the last painful agony of her mother's life. "I'm sorry." And she wiped her eyes with the back of her hand. "It's just that I never got to know her and I guess I miss her."

Meyer reached over and took her hand. She squeezed it back as though she had no intention of ever letting go.

"I was sad for a long time after she died. I finished high school, but with very little interest in learning. I dropped out of college after a year and a half, just after my father died. I didn't know what I wanted to do other than run away. So I went to Europe for a while. I lived with a family and studied art and ballet, and I traveled. I ended up staying there for five years. You know, when someone gives you enough money, you have total freedom. It can be a gift that's a curse."

"Why do you say that?"

"Money gives you the time to get confused. With enough money, you can do anything, or so I thought. But it turns out you can do nothing, too. It's taken me a long time to get going in one direction."

Meyer smiled. He was proud of her. She was candid and honest about her life and driven to become an even more worthwhile individual. "You're a fine lady. I could really get to like you."

It was 11:00 by the time they finished eating, talking and sipping wine. Meyer took her by the hand and they went into the bedroom. It was a large room with a glass door that opened on to the left side of the pool. It faced east and, even with the curtains pulled, the sun managed to shine in every morning.

Standing on the night table on the right side of the king-sized bed was a multiline telephone, an electric alarm clock and a wind-up alarm clock.

"I take it the left side is mine," Cynthia said.

Meyer nodded. "Unless you want to answer the phone in the middle of the night."

"Why two alarm clocks?"

"It's my disease. I can never be late, now. Once the electricity went off, I overslept and the O.R. canceled my case. Since then, I take no chances."

"Why don't you sleep in the O.R.?"

"Not a bad idea. I guess I could do that. I've got a case in the morning."

She smiled. "Starting tomorrow, then."

He took her by the hand again. "See this bathroom?"

She nodded.

"It's mine." Then he pointed across the room. "That one is yours. Mine has dirty underpants in the corner and whisker trimmings in the sink."

"I'm not interested in either," she said as she walked toward one of the dressers. "Which drawer do you keep your undershirts in?"

"I don't wear undershirts."

"That's not what I asked you."

"Third one down."

She opened the drawer and began looking through the pile of T-shirts. She chose one with red bands around the sleeves and collar and the letters YMCA written over the left breast. "I don't look good in plain white." And she disappeared into "her" bathroom.

Meyer walked quickly out of the master bedroom and into an adjoining smaller room that he'd fixed up as a study. The walls were covered with medical textbooks and journals. Near the far wall, but a few feet away from it, stood a massive wooden desk and behind the desk a single framed diploma from PS 102 certifying that he'd graduated from the eighth grade.

He pulled a book from the shelf behind him and began flipping through it as he sat down on the couch opposite the desk.

Cynthia stood in the doorway, watching him. Finally, she came into the room. She stood in front of him, showing herself off, her hands on her hips. "As interesting as this?"

He looked up, smiled at her and shook his head, no. She was wearing only the T-shirt, which came down to her upper thighs. Actually, it was too big for her and very little was exposed. Its looseness tried to hide her breasts.

"What are you doing?" she asked.

"Just reviewing the anatomy of the pancreas. I've got a man tomorrow with a pancreatic cancer. Just in case it's resectable, although ninety-five times out of a hundred it isn't, I want to refresh my memory."

She sat down next to him and looked over his arm. The drawings and the words were completely unintelligible to her. "How many times have you done this operation?"

"The Whipple Procedure?"

"If that's what you call it."

"Many."

"Then why are you looking it up?"

"I always do. It's a habit."

She smiled. "Another one of your mysterious diseases."

He quickly read to the end of the section and closed the book. "Cure me, then."

They went into the bedroom and Meyer took off his clothes. He'd never been shy about being naked in front of anyone. He went into the bathroom, washed and came back into the room with a towel wrapped tightly around his slim waist.

The lights were off and Cynthia was standing in front of the glass door, her body silhouetted by the yellow moonlight.

The moon was almost full, making the room bright. Meyer wondered about people who made love in the dark. When he was with someone he wanted to be with, he always made certain there was some light. The enjoyment was seeing who he was with, looking at her face, watching her responses. It was a positive feed-back system.

The only time he ever made love in the dark was when he didn't want to be there, when he wanted to use his imagination to think about someone else—when he was married.

"I love it with the moon shining in," Cynthia said as she slipped off the T-shirt. She turned slightly so that he could see her from an oblique angle.

"Do you like my body?"

"You have the most beautiful body I've ever seen," he said. "I love looking at you."

She came to him, but she didn't touch him. As they crawled under the covers, their first contact sent chills through him.

Meyer woke before either of the alarms went off, and he

held her closely. He closed the curtains just as the sun began to shine in. By the time he was dressed and ready to leave, Cynthia had fallen back to sleep and he didn't wake her.

9

As Meyer stepped away from the table, he created a momentary void that was immediately and automatically filled by the junior resident who moved up the table and assumed the position opposite Steve Foley.

As the circulating nurse unsnapped the back of Meyer's gown, he wearily flexed his shoulder muscles and pulled off the gown himself, discarding it in the linen barrel in the corner of the room. His bloody rubber gloves came off inside out and he dropped them into a waste bucket. He moved back toward the table and looked over Foley's shoulder. He stared, hypnotized by the rhythmic suturing procedure of the abdominal wall, almost unable to leave as he watched what he had seen and done thousands of times before.

"Thank you again," Foley said. "It was a great case"—he smiled under his mask—"a fabulous case."

Steve Foley was the chief resident and Michael Baum was the patient. Instead of the usual opening up, biopsying a wide-spread incurable pancreatic malignancy, perhaps performing a palliative bypass to relieve the biliary obstruction and then closing, this case was clearly Foley's fantasy come true: a Whipple Procedure, a pancreaticoduodenectomy, the rare case that chief residents dream about, even fight over.

Mr. Baum's cancer appeared localized in the head of the pancreas and, along with half the duodenum, stomach and common bile duct, it was resected. Seven hours and three anastomoses later, Mr. Baum had a chance.

Meyer looked up at the wall clock. It was 2:00 and he was late for Breast Clinic. He knew the well-oiled machinery of the clinic, which he'd worked so hard to assemble, would have no real problem without him, but Breast Clinic was special. He liked going to the meetings and he seldom missed one.

"Great job, Steve. Watch him closely." And Meyer finally turned and left.

He bought a package of chocolate chip cookies from the vending machine, went into the doctors' dressing room, poured a cup of black coffee, put his feet up on one of the couches and nursed his small food supply for a good ten minutes. He showered, dressed and walked down the corridor to the recovery room. Mr. Baum wasn't there yet, so he pushed the intercom button and talked directly with room number nine.

"Steve, this is Dr. Meyer. How's Mr. Baum?"

"Fine." Foley, his voice muffled, was obviously still at the operating table and was yelling at the call box from across the room. "We're on the skin."

Meyer took the elevator to 6-North, found Mrs. Baum in the lounge and told her what amounted to relatively good news. Then he headed downstairs to the clinic.

It was Meyer's contention that the average woman with a lump in her breast was often poorly managed. A general practitioner or gynecologist might see a patient two or three times before confirming the presence of a lump and referring the patient to a surgeon. The surgeon, in turn, would likely send the patient to a radiologist for a mammogram and then biopsy the area only if he thought it suspicious. Long delays weren't routine, but they certainly occurred with some frequency.

In the meantime, the woman with the lump in her breast was usually going through a terrible period of fear and anxiety, with no one to turn to for help. Her primary physician had sent her to a surgeon she'd never met before and the surgeon was sending her off for X rays. The families seldom had any idea of what was going on. If a patient did have breast cancer, there was little preoperative medical counseling, the therapeutic choices were seldom made clear and psychological counseling was virtually unheard of.

The whole system seemed archaic. The complex nature of breast cancer, the psychological implications in a breast-oriented society, the rapidly developing laboratory and clinical techniques, all of these suggested to Meyer that the disease would best be managed in a multidisciplinary fashion, combining the knowledge of a variety of specialists.

Once he established the clinic, he was able to obtain the services of an additional cancer surgeon, a medical oncologist and a radiation therapist, as well as a radiologist who specialized in mammography, a physician who specialized in rehabilitative medicine and a plastic surgeon to help those patients who wanted to and could be reconstructed.

In order to meet the psychological needs of the patients,

two women psychiatrists had joined the group as well as a volunteer from the American Cancer Society's Reach to Recovery Program.

Meyer had organized a system where all mental and physical treatment was represented and available in a single patient-care area, all at the same time. Other large facilities had even begun to copy the clinic's design and make-up.

He walked down the corridor of the surgical suite, past several staff members and residents and into the last room on the left. A small group was gathered around the X-ray view box, looking at mammograms.

"I think she has a time bomb on her chest," Susan Heller was saying. She looked up and saw Meyer, who, despite his six-foot-four frame, had slipped unnoticed into the back of the room. She smiled at him and went on.

Susan was presenting a case very much like her own. Meyer thought back two years to when he'd first met Susan. "A time bomb on your chest," those were his words.

Susan had already had a right mastectomy for cancer the year before he'd met her and she'd come to him seeking advice about her remaining left breast.

An additional problem was that her forty-two-year-old sister had had bilateral breast cancer and had died from it. In addition, both her mother and her aunt had had bilateral breast cancer, although they were both alive and doing well. Susan's previous breast cancer and the incredibly strong family history meant that another cancer in her remaining breast was essentially inevitable, an almost certainty.

"The risks of doing nothing are prohibitive," he'd said.

She had nodded, acknowledging that she believed him

and agreed with what he was saying. "I've got a seven-year-old son and I plan to be here to send him to Harvard, if the bastards will accept him."

He remembered laughing with her. He'd liked her immediately and a few weeks later, after their first talk, at her request, he'd performed a left simple mastectomy. It had turned out to be a good surgical judgment because, upon sectioning the breast, the pathologist had found two foci of noninvasive cancer. Probably completely curable with a simple mastectomy, it was certainly the kind of disease that if left untreated would have progressed into invasive and then, perhaps, incurable cancer.

Susan and Meyer had become good friends during her four-day hospitalization. She was up against heavy odds, not life and death odds, but the difficult odds of going back into society as a divorced, dating, sexual woman and making it work. But to Susan, breast cancer and two mastectomies had not been catastrophic setbacks. And, of course, she had made it work. A year later she'd married Louis Heller. She was incredibly strong and Meyer liked that.

As the small group filed out of the viewing room, Meyer walked up to Susan.

"You look tired," she said.

"Long case, and up late last night."

"Working?"

"No."

She smiled. "A new woman?"

He nodded and smiled back.

"Anything serious?"

"I hope not," and they both laughed. "Actually she's quite a fabulous lady."

Susan beamed. "It's about time. You need some distraction. You spend too damn much time in this hospital. Why don't you bring her over Saturday night and have dinner with us."

"That'll be great. . . . Come on and buy me coffee."

They walked down the hall and into the little storage room where the coffeepot was kept.

"I want to talk to you about me," Susan said. "About me, medically." She sipped her coffee.

"Any problems?"

"No, not really. I just want to discuss some things. . . . I'm thinking about reconstruction, but I'm not sure how I feel about it."

"Want to talk now?"

"No, in your office."

Meyer nodded. "I hate corridor consultations, too. You want to come up at the end of the day?"

"I can't. It'll keep until next week. I'll call Betty and set up a regular appointment. Now, tell me about this fabulous lady."

Rounds ended in the recovery room.

"Mr. Baum looks like a rose," Foley said. "His central venous pressure is eight, arterial pressure one hundred and thirty, hematocrit thirty-eight, blood gases are perfect, and he's putting out forty c.c.s of urine an hour. His lungs are clear. He's afebrile and fully oriented. We'll get him up and dangle him tonight."

"Good work." Meyer smiled. He walked out of the recovery room and took the elevator back to his office. He tried Cynthia's apartment, but she wasn't home. Gathering his things together, he left the hospital, rolled down both windows and headed for home. He felt good. If he'd had a little more energy, he would have taken the top off his car.

He was surprised, but happy, when he saw the yellow Morgan in his driveway.

Cynthia greeted him at the door. She hugged him and they walked into the house together.

The living room was spotless.

"What have you been doing?"

"Cleaning"—she beamed—"getting this place in order."

"Now what's my cleaning lady going to do tomorrow?"

"I was just helping her out. There's plenty left to do."

Meyer took her in his arms and kissed her on the lips.

"Thank you." She looked at her watch. "Dinner in one hour and fifteen minutes."

"Great. I'm going to run a few miles, while it's still light out."

"Have a good time. I'll be in the kitchen," and she disappeared.

He went into the bedroom, changed into a pair of shorts, a T-shirt and a pair of running shoes. He noticed a small suitcase in her bathroom. She'd probably been to her apartment.

Meyer loved to run and he'd been doing it for years. It was good exercise and since he didn't have to concentrate on a ball or other players, he could do a lot of thinking and fantasizing.

Sometimes he drove to one of the local high schools so that he could use their track. Today, he felt like running in the hills. He had carefully planned out a course that was a lot more scenic than twelve laps around a quarter of a mile oval.

He was exhilarated as he ran. Life seemed perfect: a great case in the morning; his special clinic in the afternoon; and, now, Cynthia to take care of him, to spend the evening with, to spend all night with.

This was quite an affair, he thought. He'd been dating her for three days and already she was almost living with him. They'd never really talked about it, but there was that little suitcase in the bathroom. Maybe it was all happening too fast. He thought about slowing it down, but then he decided against it. What good would that do? Steps backward never worked for him. This had felt good and right, so he'd done it. There was no reason to proceed slowly. Both of them had been there before. If one of them got hurt that was too fucking bad. That's what life was all about.

He never wanted to be on the sidelines watching others play. He was a risk taker. That's why his patients came to him; they knew he was always in there, fighting for them, never giving up, always trying to win. That was his best quality. But now that he thought about it, he really didn't live his personal life quite the same way.

Maybe he didn't want a relationship with a woman to work. But when the right woman came along, he'd always planned to marry again. With all the women he'd known over the last several years, though, it seemed hard to believe that none of them was right.

Yes, he was alone a lot, but there was a difference between being alone and being lonely. He wasn't lonely, or at least he didn't think he was. But he had to admit, it was very nice coming home and having someone like Cynthia there. But for some reason, he was beginning to feel a little crowded, even a little squeamish. He liked his personal freedom. It allowed him to make a total commitment to the hospital, to his patients and to himself. When he wanted a date, he picked up the phone and got one. The rest of the time he was free to work and that made him happy.

He was sweating profusely and he began to run even harder, clearing his mind of negative thoughts.

He lived on top of a hill and there was no way to make the last four hundred yards downhill. He walked into the house dripping wet and out of breath.

"I'm back," he yelled between gasps and he headed for the bedroom. He stripped off his wet clothes, hung them on the edge of the hamper to dry and slipped into the shower.

He stood with his eyes closed, the water beating down on his soapy body. He heard the click of the shower door opening and it startled him.

"I didn't mean to scare you," Cynthia said as she took the soap from him and began lathering his body.

"Did you see *Psycho?*"

"Yes."

"Never sneak up on anybody in a shower," he pleaded, amused.

"I'll make it up to you."

They tried to make love in the shower, but they were both so tall it was uncomfortable.

"Your choice," he said, finally, "the bed or the pool, but not the shower."

"Um, the bed now, the pool next."

They dried off, got into bed and made love. As soon as they finished, Cynthia jumped up and grabbed a T-shirt from Meyer's dresser drawer.

"I hate to fuck and run, but you men need a taste of your own medicine." She laughed. "I'll meet you in the kitchen. I don't want dinner to burn."

They had another candlelit dinner and they sat at the dining-room table for almost two hours. Meyer remembered that he really enjoyed talking and drinking coffee with someone he liked, someone he cared for.

He looked at Cynthia's beautiful face and wondered how much he'd grown since his divorce. He reached across the table and took her hand. "Thank you for being here and thank you for a lovely evening."

She smiled, a glowing smile. "Well, thank you."

"What's on for tomorrow?" he asked.

She thought for a moment. "I have classes in the morning and I'm teaching in the afternoon."

"Good. Did I tell you we're invited to dinner on Saturday?"

"No, by whom?"

"Friends of mine, Louis and Susan Heller. Susan's a doctor and Louis is a businessman. You'll like them."

She smiled. "I want to meet all your friends."

It was almost midnight when they finally went to bed. Meyer didn't think he'd ever tire of Cynthia's body. Many people wouldn't think it was perfect, but he did.

As she walked around the bedroom, naked, he just stared at her. Her breasts were too big, but they were beautifully shaped and firm. She had a small waist, perfect full hips and great legs. Her skin was smooth and creamy. There was no extra hair on her body. She was a sensuous, seductive woman. And she was completely aware of Meyer's stare.

"What part of my body do you like the best?"

"I like it all."

"I know, but if you saw me at a party, what would you notice first?"

"All of you, you're a total package."

"You know what I mean. What appeals to you the most? What part turns you on the most?"

"You have great breasts and . . ."

But she interrupted. "You don't think they're too big?"

"Not for me." He grabbed her and playfully began to stroke her breasts. The nipples became erect and he kissed them. "I also think your face and your hair are beautiful. You have great legs and a magnificent rear."

"But you like my breasts the most, don't you?"

He stopped. "Yes, I think they're the sexiest part of your body, but that's in terms of me. That's my opinion. Plenty of other men might find . . ."

"I don't care about plenty of other men." She kissed him.

The unexpected loud ring of the phone at 2:00 A.M. startled Cynthia out of a sound sleep. Her heart began beating rapidly as Jon reached over and picked up the receiver. He tried not to awaken her by shoving the receiver into his pillow so his voice would be muffled.

"Hello," he whispered.

"Dr. Meyer?"

"Yes."

"This is Steve Foley."

"Yeah, Steve."

"About an hour ago Mr. Baum dropped his blood pressure to around fifty systolic. We increased his fluids and gave him colloid. His abdomen started to swell and we gave him whole blood. He's had seven units and his pressure's about ninety."

"What do you want to do?" Holding the receiver to his ear with his shoulder and the phone in one hand while pulling a pair of underpants out of his drawer with the other, Meyer was already in motion. He knew full well that Mr. Baum had to be reoperated, but that was a decision he wanted Steve to make. Steve was the chief resident and he was the one that was going to be turned out into the community at the end of the year. He'd spent five years learning surgical judgment and Meyer was certain he wouldn't fail now.

"Well, I don't think there's much choice at this point," Steve said. "We've got to re-explore him."

"I agree." Meyer was moving quickly about the room, grabbing his pants from the chair and slipping them on. "Get him back in the O.R. as soon as you can. Tell the blood bank to try to stay at least ten units ahead of you and to try to get some fresh blood. I'm on my way." He hung up.

Cynthia was wide awake. She sensed the urgency. "What's going on?"

Meyer opened his closet and slipped on a shirt. "Oh, poor Mr. Baum, the man we operated on this morning, is bleeding into his abdomen."

"What causes that?"

Meyer calmly buttoned his shirt, pulled on his socks and slipped his feet into black loafers. "Lots of possible reasons. Perhaps a tie or a clip fell off a vessel . . . or a clot came off a vessel that we didn't tie. I don't know, but we've got to stop it."

Cynthia sat up in bed. "It's nice, you can always run out in the middle of the night and save someone's life."

"What do you mean?"

"People need you . . . what if I needed you?"

"I'd be there." He stood up and tucked in his shirt. He was ready.

She pulled the sheet up around her neck and looked carefully at him. She needed him, now. She hesitated, not wanting to upset him. "I'm afraid of what's going to happen to us . . . to me. I'm afraid of the biopsy."

He picked his car keys off the dresser and came over to the bed. "It's the middle of the night, you've just been awakened. It's dark. It's easy to be afraid. Nothing bad is going to happen to you. Don't worry and don't be afraid." He leaned over, kissed her on the cheek and left.

As he drove down the hill, he pushed the button in his car that made all four directional lights blink at once, announcing to everyone that he was speeding. He was glad that he didn't have to get up in the middle of the night and do this very often. He'd had his share, years ago, when he was still doing some general surgery. But when it did happen nothing could be more exciting.

These days it was rare for him to have to rush back into the hospital late at night. Cancer was a chronic disease, developing over a long period of time. It seldom caused problems requiring midnight surgery. Mr. Baum's bleeding was not specifically related to cancer; it could have happened after any major surgical procedure. Most middle-of-the-night cancer consultations came from patients he knew well, patients who were simply afraid. Usually, they could be taken care of over the telephone by some sympathetic listening and sensitive support.

When he hit the freeway, there was no traffic and he took the Porsche right up to a hundred miles an hour. He had a valid excuse.

By the time Meyer got to the operating room, Mr. Baum was anesthetized, his skin sutures had already been removed and the circulating nurse was prepping his protuberant abdomen. Jerry Roberts and Ann Collins were scrubbing at the sinks next to Steve Foley. They automatically moved down, allowing Meyer to scrub next to Foley.

Meyer nodded his thanks as he stepped on the rubber plunger, squirting Betadine into his hand. "Fill me in up to this point, Steve," and he rubbed the brownish antiseptic over his hands and arms. The water poured into the sink as he picked one of the coarsely bristled brushes out of the dispenser.

"He's had thirteen units of whole blood and his pressure is still below a hundred. The blood bank is about twelve units ahead of us. Only two of those are fresh, that is, drawn today. Most of them are pretty new, though. His urine output is lousy, about five c.c.s the last hour and his blood gases are bad too. He's acidotic, pH about 7.2. He's got bicarb running to counteract it."

They scrubbed for a minute rather than the ritual ten and then one by one they made their way through the swinging door and were gowned and gloved by the scrub nurse. Foley took control of the room, as Meyer wanted him to, but it was Meyer who was really in command.

As they draped the abdomen with green sheets, the tension built, time becoming the predominant factor in saving Mr. Baum's life.

In seconds the deeper sutures were cut and the old incision reopened. As they entered the peritoneal cavity, they saw nothing but old blood with its characteristic and unmistakably nauseating smell. They bailed the blood out with their hands quickly, wildly, as though they were emptying the bottom of a sinking row boat. There was nothing artistic about the procedure. It was frantic.

Pressure bags pumped blood in a steady stream into Mr. Baum through three intravenous lines. As each unit ran out, a new one was quickly inserted.

Within a minute most of the old blood was out of the belly and onto the sides of the table, the fronts of their gowns and on the floor. The circulating nurse was trying to put towels under the doctors' feet so they wouldn't slip.

New blood poured into the abdomen, almost as rapidly as old blood was being removed. The massive flow was coming from an area between the liver and the remnant of the pancreas that had been left after the first operation.

"Pressure's thirty," the anesthesiologist hollered.

"Lap pad," Foley yelled. "Another." As his hand came out of the gaping red hole, he grabbed the large sponge and feverishly returned to the abdomen. He packed the area tightly with pad after pad and the bleeding finally stopped. He held the pack firmly in position and he looked across at Meyer.

"Keep that pack right where it is," Meyer said and he breathed a sigh, but only of partial relief.

"Fifty," the anesthesiologist said. "You almost lost him. Don't do anything until I get caught up with his blood loss." He pumped the black rubber bulb, increasing the pressure on one of the units that was almost empty, and then he quickly replaced it with a full one.

Meyer looked down at Ann. "You still want to be a surgeon?"

She loosened her grip on her retractor. Her eyes were bright. "More than ever."

"Seventy," the anesthesiologist said calmly as blood continued to pour in through the darkly stained intravenous tubing.

Meyer looked at the clean, windowless tile walls. He'd spent so many hundreds, maybe even thousands, of hours in these rooms and they always looked the same, never revealing whether it was dark outside or maybe even raining. There was just no external input and he never knew or cared about what he might be missing.

Meyer and Foley talked about the next step, what they would do when Mr. Baum was stable. As they spoke, the anesthesiologist continued to infuse blood. What was going into the vascular system now was staying in.

"Pressure's a hundred and twenty," the anesthesiologist announced after about fifteen minutes. "I think you can go ahead."

"All right, let's take a look," Meyer said.

Foley slowly moved the pack. There was a large gush of blood. He quickly pushed the pack back down, stopping it.

"I think it's the medial aspect of the vena cava," Foley

said. "I couldn't tell whether it's an open vessel or just a tear, but whatever it is, it's big, because it bleeds like a son-of-a-bitch."

"How are you going to stop it?" Meyer asked.

"Let's get some pressure on the cava above and below the pack. If it's the cava, we ought to be able to control it that way."

Meyer nodded. "Go ahead."

Ann held a large Devor retractor in one hand and the lower sponge stick with the other. Jerry Roberts, who was up above Foley, held a "sweetheart" retractor on the liver and the upper sponge stick. Meyer gently held what was left of the stomach and duodenum in his right hand and the suction in his left.

"Okay, let's take a look." Foley glanced toward the anesthesiologist and his nod gave him the final go-ahead. The room was suddenly quiet except for the continual rhythmic beat of the cardiac monitor and the less frequent, more deeply pitched whoosh of the respirator.

Steve slowly loosened the pack. The bleeding was minimal and the tension rapidly dissipated. "Great," he said, "it's the cava." He pulled the pack completely out of the abdomen. "Irrigation, please."

The scrub nurse handed him a large bulb syringe filled with saline. As soon as he washed the area, he had the answer. A large tributary vein had been cut too close to the vena cava. The silk tie that had kept it closed for the last ten hours probably fell off when Mr. Baum coughed or was moved. It was a technical error that shouldn't have happened and wouldn't have had the tributary vein been cut longer and the silk suture been tied more securely.

"Give me a 5-0 vascular silk," Steve said, and he proceeded to repair the defect. He closed the hole and released the sponge sticks compressing the vein. There was no further bleeding. He inspected the rest of the abdomen. The operation they had performed in the morning was intact.

"We can close, Dr. Meyer," he said. "I can't thank you enough for coming in . . . I'm sorry this happened."

Meyer stepped away from the table. "You did a fine job, Steve, this morning and tonight. Complications are part of surgery and they happen to all of us. Good surgeons minimize them but when they happen they know what to do . . . and you're a good surgeon, Steve."

He knew Steve felt badly. Surgeons always feel badly when they have to reoperate a patient, especially when they've made a mistake. Meyer knew Steve would replay the first operation in his mind a dozen times until he did it perfectly, and then he'd never forget Mr. Baum.

Meyer walked down the corridor and into the doctors' dressing room. He took his clothes off and got into the shower. His thighs and groin were covered with Mr. Baum's blood.

It was 6:00 A.M. when he fell asleep on the couch in his office.

10

Cynthia quickly sat upright in bed and looked around the room. The sun glared in brightly through the glass door, the curtains still wide open from the night before. Jon wasn't there and he obviously hadn't come home.

She moved over to his side of the bed and picked up the phone. She stared at both alarm clocks and then dialed the hospital's main number.

"Operating room, please." She wondered whether they'd put her through. The line clicked and then began ringing.

"O.R., Miss Simpson."

"Hi. I'm calling for Dr. Meyer. He told me I could reach him here."

"I haven't seen him," Miss Simpson said.

"Oh," Cynthia mumbled.

"But our shift just came on at seven," Miss Simpson continued. "He was working all night with some of his residents, but none of them are here now. Wait a second, please."

Cynthia held on as Miss Simpson turned around and scanned the large blackboards that detailed the day's schedule for the hospital's eighteen operating rooms.

Miss Simpson came back on the line. "He's not posted for today."

"Do you know where I could find him?"

"Do what we do, page him or call his office."

"Thank you," and she hung up.

She hesitated, picked up the phone again and dialed his office number. Meyer didn't hear the ringing in his outer office and he slept soundly as one of the square buttons on the phone next to him blinked silently. After ten or twelve rings, Cynthia hung up.

She just wanted to talk to him . . . to find out how things went . . . to apologize for last night, for being scared. As a doctor he'd been through so much, so many mutilating surgeries, so many tragedies; he really didn't need to be sharing his bed with a woman who was becoming upset over a tiny breast biopsy. She wanted to say that she was sorry, that she wasn't scared.

She got up and went into the bathroom, leaving the door open so she could hear the phone if it rang. As she showered, though, her soapy hand managed to dwell on her right breast.

"Good morning," a wide-awake, bubbling Betty announced as she came into Meyer's inner office.

Meyer looked at her through one open eye.

"One black coffee, one glazed doughnut, one chocolate doughnut . . . and one extra black coffee."

Meyer sat up. "Who told you to bring me extra coffee?"

Betty smiled at him. "No one had to tell me." She

pried the top off one of the styrofoam cups and handed it to him.

"Thank you. I need this almost as much as I need to brush my teeth," and he began to sip the hot black liquid. He didn't really feel well. He wanted to be filled with energy for a new day but he was still tired from the night before. And somehow, whenever he slept on his couch, he would always wake up covered with a fine nervous sweat. He needed to go downstairs and take another shower before he could really face the day.

"I put your appointments on your desk," Betty said as she turned and left.

Meyer walked across the room, sat down, stared at his crowded schedule and began eating the glazed doughnut. He put his feet up, leaned back in his chair and closed his eyes.

He thought about Cynthia. He sat upright, dialed home and got his answering service. He dialed her number and there was no answer. He didn't know how the hell to locate her at school. He sat back, drank the other cup of coffee, ate the other doughnut and then headed downstairs to the recovery room to check on Mr. Baum.

"You're going to lose him."
Cynthia stared back at Alice Stern.
"You're rushing things, Cynthia. You're going too fast. You're just going to lose him if you keep this up."
"He's not that kind of person," Cynthia said again in protest. "He doesn't play games."
"They all play games! And believe me, they scare easily. I mean the man's thirty-eight and he's still running around.

What makes you think you're going to get him so easily? You've got to make him pursue you. It never works the other way."

Cynthia shrugged. Feminine games of hide and seek were Alice's forte and there seemed to be no way of changing her firm forty-four-year-old mind.

"I mean he sounds like a marvelous man! He could have any woman he wants. You've got to make him want you . . . chase you . . . you've got to be unattainable. He didn't say anything about tonight—fine! You shouldn't see him tonight. And you shouldn't be calling him up to ask him about it." She smiled coyly at Cynthia, obviously reading her mind.

Cynthia smiled weakly back at her.

"Michael's out of town. Why don't you come over tonight? We'll have a drink, go to dinner and who knows what else."

Cynthia shook her head. "I don't know. Jon doesn't even know where to reach me."

"That's perfect! Be mysterious. He doesn't have to know your moment-to-moment whereabouts. Let him worry about you."

Cynthia wished he would worry about her, but he seemed so confident, so in control. Nothing seemed to ruffle him.

And what about Alice? Here she was issuing orders, telling her how to handle this little love escapade. But it was so much more complicated than that! She wanted to talk to Alice . . . to tell her how she'd really met Jon. Maybe Alice would worry about her, sympathize with her, understand what she was going through. It didn't matter that the lump was benign. Right now, it was simply a terrifying unknown. She thought about discussing it with Alice. She looked carefully at her and then she rejected the idea.

"Seven-thirty at my house," Alice said.

"I'll call you at six and let you know." Cynthia stood up, picked up her tennis racket and walked into the locker rooms.

Meyer hung up the phone. He was puzzled, but in a way he was relieved. He'd just called the Neuropsychiatric Institute looking for Cynthia and he'd discovered that her dance therapy classes had been in the morning. He had a good mind for details and he was certain that she'd said "classes in the morning and teaching in the afternoon." So she'd gotten it backward. It was all right.

He liked her. He liked being with her. He liked her mind and he liked her body. But he needed a bit of time and space to himself. He was used to being alone, and when he got home tonight he was certain that all he was going to want to do was to crawl into bed, read for an hour and then go to sleep. They were going to have dinner tomorrow night, anyway. A night apart would do them both some good. By tomorrow he'd miss her even more than he missed her now.

The intercom buzzed and Betty informed him that it was already five after four and that his students were waiting in the conference room.

He put on his long white coat and walked down the corridor. Four new students would arrive on Monday morning. He was going to miss the current group, though. They'd been particularly sharp. He liked being a father figure, turning students and residents into small Jon Meyers. The more carbon copies of himself, the better medicine would be, was how he felt today.

As he walked into the conference room four smiling faces yelled out, "Surprise!"

There was a small cake in the middle of the table with one lit candle on it. The red lettering spelled out "Thanks." The coffeepot on the hot plate was full and there was a stack of white plastic cups next to it.

Meyer shook his head, then smiled. "I'm touched . . . I really am."

"This is from us," Ann said as she handed him a small box wrapped with shiny yellow paper and a piece of green wool tied in a bow.

Meyer opened the present. It was a bright red coffee mug. The bold black lettering on it spelled "Super-Surgeon."

Meyer laughed. "I love it. You know coffee's my biggest weakness."

Ann smiled. "We tried to get a cake shaped like a doughnut, but we couldn't find one."

The five of them sat around for their final hour together, the students telling Meyer their plans for the future, how good an elective he'd given them, how sad they were to leave and so on.

He pulled into his driveway about a quarter to eight. He was disappointed when he didn't see Cynthia's car.

Cynthia stared almost despondently into her half-empty coffee cup. A waiter breezed by and refilled it to the top.

"Come on," Alice said. "You've been like this all evening, and it's silly."

Cynthia looked up. "I'm sorry."

Alice picked up her purse, fiddled with it and then pulled out her American Express card.

"Let me get it." Cynthia gestured.

"Absolutely not. I invited you. But I will let you take me to Logos. You're still a member there, aren't you?"

"Yes." Cynthia nodded. "One of the few women. It's a sick place."

"Since when?"

"Since always. It just took me time to realize it. It's an expensive pick-up joint and I was dumb enough to pay to join."

"And rich enough," Alice quipped. "We'll play some backgammon, we'll go into the disco and then we'll go home."

Cynthia smiled and acquiesced. "Okay. I promise I'll cheer up."

"Where have you been, Cynthia?" Robert, the maître d' at Logos, seemed overjoyed to see her. "You just disappear for three months without even telling anyone," and he put his arm around her. He wore an open shirt with a lot of gold jewelry around his neck and black tight pants.

"Can you get us a backgammon table, Robert?" Cynthia asked, and she proceeded to lose seven straight games. A number of men who didn't know her came up to offer their intellectual assistance. She declined. A number of men who did know her offered their best smiles.

"Your mind is not on the game," Alice finally conceded and they went into the disco area.

The brown suede chairs swallowed them up as they sat and watched, trying unsuccessfully to become observers in the dimly lit room. The dance floor was alive with the rhythm of music, with svelte bodies sensually swaying. Cynthia finally said yes to someone and became a part of it. Alice watched her, admiring her natural rhythm. She seemed completely fluid, dancing as well as she walked and talked. She was one of the few people who belonged on the dance floor, Alice thought.

The man came back with Cynthia, sat down and began to talk. She looked at him, not hearing a word, only listening to the music, sipping her white wine and trying not to think. She couldn't imagine herself looking any differently . . . she didn't want to think.

All of a sudden, she couldn't stand being there. She grabbed Alice by the arm and they left.

Turning left on Santa Monica Boulevard, she drove into the residential section of Beverly Hills, made a right on Alice's street and dropped her off. Then she continued north to Sunset Boulevard and stopped in the left-turn lane. When the light changed, she quickly looked behind her, changed her mind and made a sweeping right going east, away from the ocean.

She drove for a while, then turned left and went up into the hills. What if he had another girl there? She really should have called, but it was so late and he was probably asleep already. She drove slowly. Twice she almost changed her mind and turned around. Finally, she pulled into

Meyer's driveway. Only his car was there, and the house was dark.

She walked around to the left side by the kitchen and tried the back door. It was open. Carefully she made her way through the house and into the bedroom. She felt like a thief as she bumped into furniture, and she was frightened. She peered into the bedroom. He was alone. She stripped her clothes off and slipped silently into the bed, trying not to wake him.

He sat up abruptly, issuing a guttural moan.

She grabbed him. "It's me, Cynthia. Don't be frightened."

He put his arms around her. "You scared the hell out of me."

She patted him and rubbed his neck and back. "I'm sorry."

"What time is it?"

"Almost two."

He looked over at the clocks. "I've been asleep for five hours already." He got out of bed, went to the bathroom and came back with a lighted candle. "We'd better talk." He smiled at her as he crawled back into bed.

Cynthia liked looking at his naked muscular body in the candlelight. She confessed that she had been playing hard to get, avoiding him.

He laughed and told her how he'd wanted to be alone and yet how disappointed he'd felt when her car wasn't in his driveway and how tonight, without her, he'd felt lonely.

"I was afraid there might be another girl here."

He put his arms around her and changed the subject. He told her how well Mr. Baum was doing. The story of the "midnight save" excited her and she was proud to be with him.

They lay naked in bed together and talked a little longer. Feeling close to one another, they made gentle, sweet love, less passionate than before, but nice.

11

Meyer made it home from the hospital by 11:30. He went from the living room to the kitchen and then out onto the sun deck. He opened the sliding glass door and went into the bedroom.

"Cynthia," he called out.

"In here." She was sitting at the desk in his study, a book open in front of her.

"What are you doing?"

"Just reading some of your books. Where did you disappear to this morning?"

He came around to the side of the desk, kissed her on the cheek and then sat down on the couch. "I went to grand rounds. We have them every Saturday morning." He put his feet up on the wooden coffee table in front of him.

"I thought you were taking the weekend off."

"I am, from now until tomorrow night."

"That's what you call a weekend off?"

Meyer grinned.

Cynthia closed the book she was reading and put it back on the shelf with the dozens of other volumes on cancer. "It's nice to have a room of your own. I have a room, I didn't show it to you."

"Why not?"

"It's private." She smiled. "It's also kind of messy. It's got a mirror and a barre for dancing, my needlework, my paints and a lot of other things."

"You should have shown it to me. I'd like to see your creations."

"You will. Oh, by the way, some fellow named Paul Cutler called; he claims he's your best friend and that you've been neglecting him."

Meyer laughed. It sounded exactly like what Paul Cutler would have said to an unknown female voice. "He is and I have been."

"Well, he and someone named Maryann are coming over for lunch."

"Good. How did that get arranged?"

"I'm not sure. He's a very good talker. Either I invited him spontaneously or he invited himself and made me think I did."

"Probably the latter," Jon said. "He's a fancy Beverly Hills lawyer and he gets paid to make people think his words are theirs."

"He sounded nice."

"You'll like him. He's a brilliant fellow, a little crude every now and then. He's short, about five three, with a mop of curly brown hair and a full beard. He looks like a rabbi or a heroin pusher. Is he bringing his kids?"

"He didn't say anything about them."

"Probably not, then," Meyer said. "He only gets them on Sundays and Wednesdays. What time are they coming?"

"About one."

Meyer looked at his watch. "We've got an hour." He walked amorously toward Cynthia.

"Wrong! You've got an hour to clean up the deck and get the leaves out of the pool. I'm going into the kitchen."

By 2:30 in the afternoon the four of them were sitting around the redwood table having their third or fourth cups of coffee. Cynthia had no problem relating to Jon's friends. She liked Paul and Maryann. Right away she'd felt exceptionally comfortable with them.

"How did you ever get involved with the Neuropsychiatric Institute?" Maryann asked. "I teach sixth graders and they're almost more than I can handle."

Cynthia smiled. "I took some psychology courses years ago, when I was first in college. And I'd taken dancing lessons from the time I was six. I'd always used dance as a method of expressing my own feelings and I thought patients might like to try it. A year or so ago I was playing tennis with a woman whose husband is a psychiatrist. He let me work with some of his patients and, finally, it became a job."

"It sounds as difficult as Jon's work."

"It's worse," Jon chimed in. "Cancer is curable. We cure at least a third of all cancer patients."

"So you're trying to tell me I'm lucky," Paul said.

"If you get a neurologic disease like multiple sclerosis or you have a heart attack, you're never cured. These schizophrenic kids that Cynthia works with are seldom cured."

Cynthia looked at Paul. "What do you mean, 'lucky'?"

"Didn't Jon tell you how we met?"

"No, not really."

"We met at a party. I found out that he was a big surgeon so I thought I'd get some free medical advice and show him a bump on my arm. To make a long story short, I had a fatty cancer, a liposarcoma, and Jon removed it. Cured me, so he says. I wouldn't pay his bill and we became the best of friends."

Cynthia stared down at the skin graft covering the flat wide depression on Paul's forearm. He stretched it forward giving her a better look. "Ugly, isn't it?"

"It's not ugly," Jon protested.

Paul chuckled. "You're so touchy when it comes to your work. You know I'm only kidding." He reached over and squeezed the back of Jon's neck. "What would I do without my friend." He smiled, and looked over toward Cynthia, trying to make amends. "He's the best there is and I'm serious about that."

"I know that," she said. "I'm even going to let him operate on me."

Suddenly, she felt relieved. She had blurted it out to two almost complete strangers. She turned toward Jon. "But I don't want one of those skin grafts," she laughed.

"What are you going to operate on, Jon?" Paul asked. "You can't improve this woman."

"It's personal," Jon replied.

Cynthia looked at Paul. "I have a small lump in my breast and Jon is going to remove it. That's how we met. Almost like the two of you."

Paul frowned and turned toward Jon. "Are you crazy, Jon? You don't operate on your friends."

His comment stunned Cynthia. Where was Paul's support for her? His empathy? Weren't their situations similar? "He operated on you and you're his friend," she said.

"We weren't friends when he operated on me and it seems to me that a lump in the arm is a lot different from something in the breast."

"What if your lipo, whatever it was, came back?"

"Of course, I'd want to have Jon take care of me. But my case is different. Sarcomas are a very rare cancer. I'd want someone with Jon's experience."

"Well, so do I."

"Stop," Jon interrupted. He wiped his forehead. "How do I get myself into these messes? First of all, Paul, if, God forbid, you ever had a recurrence, I wouldn't want to operate on you. Being an effective surgeon takes a certain amount of detachment and I don't have that with you anymore. I'd try like hell to get someone who shared my opinion on how you should be treated and I'd take care of you only if I was forced to, if there was no one else competent around, and that's highly unlikely nowadays."

He turned toward Cynthia, hesitating. "I don't really want to operate on you either, Cynthia. I'm much too involved with you. I want to ask someone else to do your case."

"You never told me that, Jon." She stared at him.

Jon looked down. "I'm sorry, Cynthia." He reached out for her hand, but she pulled it away. "I just never thought of it when we were together. I'm sorry."

"Who is going to operate on me?" she asked, stunned. "Don't you think I have a right to know, to choose?"

"Of course, but this isn't the place to discuss it." He looked at Paul and Maryann. "Would you excuse us for a while?" He got up and took Cynthia by the arm. "Why don't you two put your bathing suits on and we'll join you later."

In the study he sat down next to Cynthia on the couch and told her of his tentative plans to ask Ted Stoner to do the biopsy.

"How could you even think of asking him without asking me first?"

"Cynthia, believe me, it just slipped my mind. Don't make a big thing out of it."

"To me it is a big thing. It's my body and my breast and it's goddamn important." She couldn't help it, she started to cry. "I picked you, you were supposed to be my surgeon."

Jon put his arms around her. "Please don't worry." Then he handed her a tissue. "I care about you. I've never faced a situation like this and I guess I used bad judgment. But you've got to forgive me and not make it worse than it is. Stoner is an excellent surgeon. He generally makes the same incision around the nipple that I do, so you're not really going to have a scar. I'm sure you'll like him. I'll set it up for you to see him on Monday, and if you agree, he can do the surgery on Thursday in the original time slot that I had scheduled."

"What if I don't like him?"

"Then I'll find someone that you do like." He was feeling terrible. "Whatever you want."

"No matter who does the biopsy, I want you there."

"A breast biopsy is a simple operation. The reason I want Ted to do it is because I don't want to be involved with any decision-making regarding your case. It's not good for you or for me."

"What decision-making is there? You said it was benign."

"It is, but I wouldn't even want to watch a dentist filling your tooth or someone sticking a needle into you and giving you Novocaine. Doesn't that make sense?"

"It makes sense, but everybody says you're the best."

"Nobody's the best when it comes to a breast biopsy. A resident can do it as well as I can."

"Will you just be there?" she pleaded.

"I'll be there," he conceded.

She hesitated. "What if I ever needed one of the bigger operations, would you help?"

"If that's what you wanted, yes, I'd help. But I don't think you'll need anything more than a biopsy."

She put her arms around him and held him tightly. "I need you now," she whispered. "Please make love to me."

While Jon respected her for demanding what she wanted, he was upset that she'd made him feel guilty and she'd made him promise to be there. He'd promised to do something he didn't want to do, something totally unnecessary. Yet, her closeness excited him and he was amazed at how easily he could respond to her. They made love on the couch.

Cynthia came out of the house wearing a brief two-piece string suit.

Paul sat up. "I didn't think you were ever coming back, but this was certainly worth waiting for."

Cynthia grinned. "My suit?"

"No, your body. Maryann, why don't you get a suit like that?"

Maryann looked at Paul. "Why don't you try out for the Lakers?"

After about twenty minutes in the sun, Cynthia took off her top and dove into the pool. She swam a dozen laps, got out and put on a short terry-cloth robe.

"Does anyone want anything from the kitchen?" she asked.

Meyer and Paul both wanted beers and Maryann went in to help.

"Great tits," Paul whispered.

Jon made a face. "Come on, Paul."

"Since when does the word 'tits' offend you?"

"I've never liked the word and I particularly don't like it in reference to Cynthia."

"I apologize, then. She has magnificent breasts."

"She's a beautiful woman," Jon agreed, "in a lot of ways."

"How long have you known her?"

"About a month. We've only been dating for five days, though."

"A typical Jon Meyer blitzkrieg." Paul smiled. "But she's lasted longer than most and that's good because I like her. Have you settled this biopsy business?"

"No problem."

"Nothing serious, I hope."

"No."

By 4:30 Paul and Maryann were leaving. As Jon walked them to their car, Maryann whispered to him, "You know, I had a nice long talk with Cynthia. She's a lovely person. I think she's very sensitive about this biopsy business and a little overanxious to please you. So be good to her and give her a chance. She's the best person I've ever seen you with."

12

The evening really hadn't been going well. Cynthia found it difficult to concentrate, difficult to become part of the conversation. Louis and Susan Heller were certainly nice enough people and they were very interesting, but for some reason Cynthia couldn't open up to either of them. Jon and the Hellers seemed to belong together. She felt separated from them and it was clearly her fault. She just hadn't quite been able to recover since early in the afternoon when Jon had made his announcement about another surgeon.

Then there was Susan, another surprise. Cynthia had walked in the door, smiling, and she'd recognized Susan as the radiologist who had done her xeromammograms. Susan remembered her, too. Now, whenever she looked at Susan or Jon, she was reminded of the biopsy. It was all she could seem to think about. She struggled, internally, to appear grown up and brave. She tried to rid her mind of what was becoming an abundance of obsessive thoughts, but she kept failing.

"Can I help you?" she asked, as Susan began picking up the dessert plates. Automatically, Cynthia stood and began collecting things from her side of the table. She followed

Susan into the kitchen, piling what she was carrying into the sink. As she turned to leave, Susan took her gently by the arm.

"Let's sit down for a second. I want to talk with you. The men have enough coffee for a while."

"Sure."

They sat at a small round table in the corner of the kitchen and poured two fresh cups of coffee.

"What's the matter?"

Cynthia shrugged. "Nothing."

Susan shook her head, no. "It's something. I don't know you very well, but you're not yourself. Is it this biopsy thing?"

Cynthia nodded, yes.

"I kind of know what's been going on. When you were talking with Louis, I bawled out Jon for dating a patient. He told me you weren't his patient anymore and what had happened today, about switching doctors. He's done the right thing, but he did it the wrong way."

"Somehow I almost feel *abandoned*. I know it's silly."

"You're not abandoned. You and I can talk about it. I'll be around all next week. I know Dr. Stoner and I agree with Jon, he's excellent."

"It's begun to terrify me. What if I do have cancer?"

"Jon says he doesn't think you do and I didn't see anything on your mammograms. I'm sure that everything will be all right."

Cynthia tried smiling as she talked with Susan about her life, about where she'd been, what she'd done and how much she'd wanted a man like Jon. And then she confessed. "I lied to him. I told him I was back in college, because that's what I'd like to be doing. It's something I *want* to do, and I'm ready to do, but I just haven't quite done it yet."

"I understand," Susan said. "But you don't have to lie to Jon. It doesn't matter to him. I'm sure of that. Just tell him the truth . . . trust him."

"But why didn't he tell me about his plans? Why didn't he trust me to help with the decision?"

"It was wrong," Susan said again. "But it's over and done with and I don't think it was a question of trust or lack of trust. Try to get it out of your mind."

"I can't. I keep thinking the worst. What if I do have breast cancer? What if I lose a breast?"

"It's a terrible experience, but it's not the end of the world," Susan reasoned. "Women go on."

"Who'd want me with one breast?"

"Who'd want me with none?"

"What?"

"None," Susan said again. "Look at me. I've had cancer in both breasts." She held her hands up to the two small protuberances on her chest. "These aren't real. They're silicone bags in my bra."

Cynthia was stunned. She looked at Susan, her eyes wide open.

"I went on. Someone wanted me. I married Louis after my second breast was removed. It's not a nice thing and I went through hell, but it's not the worst thing people have to face. I'm still alive. I have my son and now Louis." She looked at Cynthia. "You're a fabulous woman. You're smart and you're very talented and creative. There's so much to you. Don't let your beautiful body blind you to the rest of your assets." She reached across the table and Cynthia took her hand. "But it's okay to feel scared. It's normal."

Cynthia had tears in her eyes. She wanted Susan to be her friend.

"As soon as the biopsy is done and everything is all right, you'll be yourself again. Just like magic. And then you can go about the business of your life. I think you and Jon make a wonderful couple. I have very good feelings about it."

13

Cynthia Rogers was twenty minutes late for her appointment on Monday with Ted Stoner. It was his first day back from vacation and he didn't usually see patients on Mondays. If it weren't for the fact that he was doing Meyer a personal favor, he wouldn't have waited to see her.

In his late forties, Stoner's slenderness gave him a youthful appearance that was counterbalanced by his graying hair; his eyes were cold gray-blue.

He looked carefully over Cynthia's brief records. "Not much here." Finally, he smiled at her, stood up and guided her toward the examining room. He confirmed the presence of the mass and then reviewed her xeromammograms.

"What has Dr. Meyer told you about this lump?"

"He said there was a lump, it wouldn't go away and it should be removed . . . and that he thought it was benign."

"I agree completely," Stoner said, nodding. "Now, you know that surgery has been set up for Thursday morning. So we'll plan on bringing you in on Wednesday."

"Jon said that if I wanted, the mass could be removed

under local anesthesia, and I wouldn't have to stay overnight in the hospital."

"Well," Stoner said, "that's one of Dr. Meyer's favorite tricks. He likes to do all his breast biopsies under local. I think that's fine for him and I do it when it's appropriate. However, some breast biopsies are hard to do that way and I think yours would be one of them. You have a very big, firm breast and the mass is situated quite deeply. I could do it under local, but there would be some pain. I also think that it might be fairly difficult to control any bleeding that occurred." He tried to look warm and supportive. "I'd rather put you to sleep for this one."

She was relieved. "I'm kind of glad. I think I'd rather be asleep. I was going to let Jon do it his way because I knew he'd be angry if I didn't. But the thought of it made me uneasy."

"Don't worry about Dr. Meyer," Stoner said. "I'm taking care of you now. The first decision is made, then; you'll have general anesthesia. Now, the second question is whether or not we do anything at the same time, if we should find cancer. Has Dr. Meyer explained this to you? Has he told you about frozen sections and the different operations, the one-stage and the two-stage procedures?"

"Yes," Cynthia said. "He showed me a whole series of pictures and he told me the difference between each operation. I never really reached a decision since he wanted to do the biopsy under local," she said. "If it turned out to be anything, we'd discuss what to do the next day, and then I'd come in for a second operation." She added quickly, "But I never agreed to that."

"Have you given any thought to which operation you'd want if the lump were cancer?"

Cynthia looked away from him. "My mother had breast cancer, I don't want to be deformed."

"If the biopsy shows cancer," Stoner said, "I think that I ought to go ahead, right then and there, and perform a mastectomy."

Cynthia didn't want to look at him.

"I think that a modified radical would be the best procedure for you," Stoner continued. "It would leave your muscle intact and you'd look pretty good in clothes. If you wanted, later, you could be reconstructed."

"Will that leave some of the breast?" Cynthia asked.

"No, that's a partial mastectomy and I don't think Dr. Meyer would recommend that either."

Stoner decided to pitch the modified radical hard, and he touted the one-stage operation as being the right way to go. For him it was no different than selling encyclopedias.

"What's the sense of two separate hospital admissions, two general anesthesias and two operations? If it's cancer, you're going to have to get it taken care of, so you might as well do it all at one time. It's a hell of a lot simpler that way. We'll do a complete metastatic work-up on Wednesday and I can assure you"—he leaned back in his chair—"I'll do nothing radical on Thursday unless the pathologist is absolutely certain. The odds are that this lump is benign. We just want to be prepared."

"And Jon is going to be there?" Cynthia asked.

"If that's what you'd like and he's willing."

Cynthia was convinced. Biopsy under general anesthesia, frozen section pathological diagnosis and modified radical mastectomy if the frozen section was unequivocally malignant. This wasn't the way Jon would have done it, but it was her body and her life and this was what she wanted.

She walked down the hallway to Jon's office. When she told him what she'd decided, he was furious.

"Didn't anything I explained to you before sink in?"

"It all did," she said, "but you sent me to a different doctor and he convinced me that, for me, his viewpoint was correct."

"I thought you shared my feeling that women need to participate in decisions about their own bodies."

"I do," she said, "and I helped make this decision. I didn't make it clear to you before, but I was very apprehensive about having the biopsy done under local anesthesia. When Dr. Stoner said that he'd rather do it with me asleep, that was all I needed. He's my doctor now and I've got to trust him."

"Goddamn it!" Jon almost shouted. Then he stopped himself. Plenty, in fact, most breast biopsies throughout the United States were being done every day under general anesthesia. The reason he sent Cynthia to Ted Stoner was so that Stoner could make the decisions and yet here he was still trying to run the show.

"What if it's malignant?" he continued. "Are you sure you want to go right ahead with the definitive operation without talking it over first?"

"I don't see any point in waiting. I'd have to have it sooner or later. I might as well have it all in one sitting." Then she looked at him. "Don't worry, Jon. It's benign."

"Jesus Christ! You and Stoner are setting breast surgery back ten years."

"Enough! I'm in good hands and the decision is made. Isn't that what you wanted, someone else to make the medical decisions for you?" She didn't wait for his answer. "You're not involved anymore."

Jon felt completely frustrated. "You're right." He looked down at his watch. "I'm late for rounds."

"How's Mr. Baum?" she asked. She didn't want him to leave.

"He's doing pretty well."

She smiled. "I'm glad."

"Why don't I come by and see you on Wednesday night after you've had your tests and you're all settled in your room?"

"That's it?" she asked. "You don't want to see me before then?"

"I didn't say that. It's just that I won't be out of here until ten tonight, and tomorrow night I've got Journal Club with the residents. Maybe it's better if we just get this goddamn biopsy over with."

"You're angry at the way I've decided to do it."

"Yes, I'm angry. Let's just get it the hell out of the way."

She was stunned. After six intensely involved days together, he was suddenly treating her as if he hardly knew her.

"What do you want me to say? That I don't care how it's done and that I'll do it your way?"

"I don't want you to say anything." He looked down at his watch again.

"Are you angry about what I told you yesterday? About my lying to you?"

"Of course not," Meyer said. "Yesterday was a beautiful

day together. Whether you go to school or not is something you're going to have to work out for yourself."

"It seems I have to work everything out for myself."

"What do you mean by that?"

"You don't seem to be able to tell when someone needs you."

Meyer looked at her, not really understanding what she was saying. "I guess I'm not a very good doctor at home."

Cynthia stood up. "I don't need a doctor . . . I need a friend."

Meyer walked her to the elevator, waited until it came, said good-bye and then hurried down the hall.

He bumped into Ted Stoner, who was rounding with Michael Benedict, his resident, and Ann Collins. Ann smiled brightly at Meyer.

"I saw your lady friend this afternoon," Stoner said.

"Thanks, Ted, I want to talk to you about her."

Stoner turned to Michael Benedict. "Why don't you two go ahead? I'll catch up to you in a few minutes." As they left, he turned back toward Meyer.

"Ted, I'm not sure I should be in the operating room when you do Cynthia's biopsy. I feel I should be completely out of it."

"I couldn't agree with you more," Stoner answered. "But she says you promised her that you'd be there. I'll try to talk her out of it when she comes in. But if she still wants you in the operating room, then I think you're obliged, particularly if she has a mastectomy."

"That brings me to another point," Jon said. "Do you think it's wise to do her in a single stage if by some chance she does have cancer?"

"Sure. I don't see any reason not to."

"Well, she's an emotional woman. She's very tied up with her body, particularly her breasts."

"I don't blame her," Stoner said. "She's got a fine body and I think it would be abnormal for her not to be involved with it."

"I know that, but it's a question of degree. I think she's extremely involved with her body and the loss of a breast would be devastating to her."

"It is to most women," Stoner said.

"I think it would be worse in this case."

"That's probably true," Stoner agreed, "but she's fully informed as to what the choices are and she's made her own decision."

"Ted, you know that's bullshit. You made the decision and sold it to her."

"Isn't that what I'm supposed to do?" he asked. "That's what informed consent is—telling the patient everything and then getting her to buy what you're selling, what you believe is best."

"Maybe that's what it is to you, but in this particular case, Ted, you may have sold the wrong package."

"If there's so much emotional overlay, don't you think it's better to get the whole thing over with in a single shot? What good will it do if she does have cancer and she waits around for three or four days trying to make the same decision that she's already made?"

"I agree, those wouldn't be the best few days in her life. But what I've discovered is that most women sign for a single-stage operation just to please the doctor. When they're scared they really don't listen to the alternatives and they're not always making the best possible choice for themselves. Most breast biopsies are benign, so why do we put them through so much emotional pain for no reason? When you talk to a patient like Cynthia, before she's had her biopsy, nothing's for real. It's all conjecture. It's a lump that could be cancer, but most likely it isn't. Who knows? But everything is different if you just do the biopsy, get the results and then make the decision. That way, when you're dealing with cancer, both you and the patient know it. That's what makes the difference."

"I really don't think it makes much difference," Stoner said, "but I'll ask her again when she comes in Wednesday. I'll tell you now though, I'm not anxious to do any woman in two stages. It wastes a lot of time—two operations, two anesthesias. It's a pain in the ass."

"I'm sorry you feel that way, Ted, but that's the future. Five years from now women won't accept what you're offering. They're going to demand to play a major role in the care of their own bodies. And just about every goddamn breast case is going to be done in two stages, with the first stage, incidentally, done under local anesthesia."

"I didn't think local would be a good idea in Cynthia's case," Stoner said. "Her breast is too big and the lesion is too deep."

"If you wanted to, Ted, you could do it. You're an excellent technical surgeon."

"You're right," Stoner raised his voice. "If I wanted to. I thought you sent her to me so that you wouldn't have to be involved in the decision-making."

"I did."

"All right, then stop being involved. She's in good hands."

"Let me say one more thing," Meyer hesitated. "If that lump turns out to be cancer, I'd seriously consider a partial mastectomy in Cynthia's case."

Stoner looked disdainfully at Jon. "I can't believe you said that." And he turned and walked down the hall.

14

On Wednesday, Cynthia stood alone in front of the window in her living room. The glass was covered with a thin layer of dust. The harsh light from the sun glared through the filmy haze and she could see her own blurred image in the reflection.

She turned away and put her cigarette out in one of the plants closest to her. She retrieved it quickly, turned from the window and whispered to the plant:

"I'm sorry."

She wandered around the apartment, picking dead leaves off the plants and then giving them water. She stepped over the pillows that were strewn about the room and over the trash that had accumulated over the last two days. The phone rang, but she didn't answer it.

She picked up her small suitcase and walked out to the car.

Jon was just like her father, she thought. He could never love anyone. Her father had punished her all her life by not loving her enough, and she had been repeating the pattern over and over again by being with men who couldn't love her, or anyone else for that matter.

But Jon could love: he loved his patients and his students. Why had he abandoned her now, when she needed him so much?

She kept thinking about him as she drove to the hospital.

It was 8:30 Wednesday night when Jon walked into room 617. Cynthia was under the covers of her bed reading a magazine. She was wearing a pink nightgown.

"Hi," he said. "How are you?"

"I'm fine," she said coldly. "Dr. Stoner has already been here. He told me that you tried to change his mind about how he should do my operation."

"I told him my point of view."

"You could do me a favor by staying out of it. I've already made the decision and that's the way it is. If I have anything bad, I want it all taken care of tomorrow morning."

"If that's your decision and you've honestly thought it through and made it, that's fine. I won't argue."

"That is my decision."

It was quiet for a few seconds. Cynthia looked at Jon. "Dr. Stoner doesn't think it's cancer either, but he wasn't as certain as you were."

"We have different personalities."

"You're going to be there tomorrow, aren't you?" she asked.

"I'd rather not be, but if you want me to, I will."

"I want you to, you promised."

"I know I promised, and I'll be there if that's what you want. It's just going to be emotionally hard for me to watch someone making an incision into your body, even if it's just a tiny biopsy incision."

What he was saying seemed inconsistent to Cynthia. Where had he been "emotionally" for the last two days?

"I'm glad you'll be there," and she held out her hand.

He took it. The anger that had been in her voice when he'd first entered the room was gone. They looked at each other for a long moment.

"I'll see you in the morning in the operating room." He started to leave.

"Wait a minute." She couldn't let him go.

But he didn't know quite what to say. He was feeling badly about the last two days. Here he was, the caring doctor, and he couldn't care for someone he really knew, someone he really liked. He'd wanted her to be strong, not to need him. But maybe those were big demands for a young woman who was obviously afraid of breast cancer. He knew she would be all right, but he'd been through this so many times before and she hadn't.

Finally he spoke. "Cynthia, I was wrong not to be with you for the last few days."

She held his hand tightly and looked directly at him.

"I was wrong and I admit it. I've been a lousy friend and I'm sorry. I do care about you."

"I needed you," she said softly. "I was scared."

"I didn't want you to be scared."

"I can't be something just to please you."

"I know that. But I guess I was scared, too . . . scared that we were getting too close."

"That was so foolish. . . . You could have helped me by just being there, letting me have someone to share my feelings with. . . . We were both afraid and there was nothing to be afraid about."

He nodded and he understood. He bent down and kissed her. "Good night. I'll see you in the morning and try not to worry. It's going to be fine."

15

Meyer didn't sleep well and he came into the hospital early on Thursday morning. He went to his office, put on a long white coat and then took the elevator down to the cafeteria.

It was rare for him to eat a regular breakfast. But today, in addition to his coffee and doughnuts, he ordered bacon and eggs. He wasn't at all hungry and he ate the food mechanically, almost neurotically, like a fat person. Two other doctors on the staff joined him, but he wasn't in a talkative mood. As soon as he finished, he excused himself.

Why was he so uptight? he wondered. He wasn't doing the biopsy. He wasn't making the decisions. He had no responsibility. All he had to do was show up.

He walked into the operating suite, nodded to everyone who said hello to him and finally arrived at the doctors' dressing room. As he finished changing, Ted Stoner walked in and they exchanged "Good mornings."

Meyer scanned the three large blackboards at the main desk which detailed all the cases that were scheduled for the day. He looked down the list to room five. The first case was at 7:30. He read across the line: "Patient—Rogers; room 617-N; Surgeon—Stoner; Assistant—Meyer/Benedict;

Operation—Rt. Breast Bx, FSMRIM [right breast biopsy, frozen section, modified radical if malignant]; Anesthesia—general; Anesthesiologist—Paley."

One line told it all.

He went down to room five and walked in. "Good morning," he said and went to the operating table in the center of the room. "Hi," he whispered as he reached under the sheets and squeezed Cynthia's hand.

She looked at him. "Jon. Wow, am I sleepy. Happy, too. Not afraid at all." She smiled.

Cynthia was well premedicated, Meyer thought. The morphine had done its job. She could easily have been done under local.

"I'm glad," Jon said softly.

Just then Ted Stoner came into the room. He was the surgeon of record and he would run the room. "Okay, let's get going." As Michael Benedict left the room to begin scrubbing, Stoner turned to Ann. "You don't have to scrub on the biopsy." He walked over to Cynthia and Meyer backed away. "Hi, it's Dr. Stoner."

"Hi, Dr. Stoner."

"We're going to start now; it'll all be over in a few minutes." He turned and walked out of the room.

Ann Collins moved back into the corner, out of the way and next to Meyer. "She's a friend of yours?"

"Yes." Meyer volunteered no other information. He seemed preoccupied and Ann elected not to ask him any other questions or to comment on her first week with Stoner.

The anesthesiologist had already started an intravenous in Cynthia's left hand. Everything was ready. Dr. Paley injected Sodium Pentothal into the IV tubing and in seconds Cynthia was asleep. He put a mask on her face and announced that he was not going to put an endotracheal tube into her windpipe during the biopsy. He would put the tube in later if it turned out that she needed to have a mastectomy.

Once she was asleep, the circulating nurse came over to the table and pulled down the top sheet, exposing Cynthia's naked body.

All during this time Ted Stoner and Michael Benedict had been scrubbing at the sink and talking about the case that was scheduled to follow Cynthia. It was far more interesting than a breast biopsy.

The circulating nurse put on a pair of sterile rubber gloves and began to prep the biopsy site. Using a Betadine-soaked sponge forcep, she made ever-enlarging concentric circles until the entire breast was covered with the yellow-brown antiseptic solution.

Meyer didn't bother to scrub for the biopsy. It would be ridiculous, he thought: two fully trained, board-certified surgeons, as well as a second-year surgical resident; all scrubbed on a ten-minute breast biopsy of a benign lump. Ridiculous.

As Stoner and Benedict came back into the operating room, each one was handed a towel and each one dried his hands and arms as he had hundreds of times in the past. Both were gowned and gloved by the scrub nurse.

Then they placed four green towels in a square around Cynthia's right breast. Over this they placed a folded green sheet. As they opened it, it covered her entire body except for the hole through which her glistening yellow-brown breast protruded. The breast was now totally dissociated from the body and the operation could begin.

"Knife," Stoner called out.

The scrub nurse passed him a scalpel with a number ten blade.

"No," he said as he passed it back, "I want a smaller blade. Put a fifteen on there."

She did as she was told and gave the scalpel back to him.

He made a small, curved incision, perhaps an inch long, at the junction of Cynthia's sun-tanned skin and her areola. He carried the incision through the full thickness of skin.

"Buzzer," he said. And the scrub nurse passed him the electrocoagulating unit. He cauterized a few small bleeding vessels and the field was completely dry.

"Metzenbaum scissors and toothed forceps, and give Dr. Benedict a small Richardson retractor."

Stoner lifted up the upper skin edge and undermined it with a few deft movements of his scissors. He pushed his finger into the hole he'd created, felt for a few seconds and said, "Here it is. Way in here." He placed Dr. Benedict's retractor in the wound. "Hold this."

"An Allis clamp, please."

He placed the clamp deep into the breast tissue and began to cut around it. He stopped and felt again. "It'll be out in a second. Notify pathology."

The circulating nurse pushed the intercom button on the wall. A green light went on as the little box made a pinging sound. A female voice answered, "Pathology."

"This is room five," the nurse said, "we have a frozen for you."

The voice answered, "Thank you," and the green light went out.

At that moment Ted Stoner made the final snip with his scissors. "It's out. Give me a clean knife, I want to look at it."

He took the fresh knife and cut the mass open. "It's funny-looking," he said. "A bit suspicious in one area, but I doubt it. Let's see what the pathologist has to say."

He handed the specimen off the table and Meyer looked at it carefully. "I think it's a benign fibroadenoma. They often look like this."

"I agree," Stoner said. "Let's close while they're doing the frozen." The specimen was taken from the room to pathology and Stoner cauterized a few more bleeding vessels.

"Five-o nylon," he said. "She'll never know she had an operation." He completed the plastic closure in about two minutes.

Meyer looked over Ted's shoulder. It was a fine job.

"What the hell's keeping those guys?" Stoner asked. "All they have to do is sit on their asses and look at a slide."

He pulled the drapes off Cynthia's naked sleeping body and told Michael Benedict to put a dressing on the biopsy site. He took off his gown and gloves and turned to Meyer. "As soon as we hear that it's official, you can buy me a coffee."

The green light on the wall went on with the same pinging noise it had made earlier. A male voice said, "Dr. Stoner?"

Ted walked over to the intercom. "Yes?"

SIDE EFFECTS

The voice said, "This is Dr. Nadi in pathology. Can you hear me?"

"Yes," Stoner hollered back.

The voice spoke. "This tumor is an infiltrating ductal carcinoma."

Meyer's eyes widened. He felt a sharp pain in his chest and his heart began to beat rapidly. His armpits and hands were instantly wet.

"You must be kidding!" Stoner shouted. "Who else has seen it?"

"I've shown it to Dr. Oswald and Dr. Foreman," the voice said. "They agree. There's no question about it. It's invasive cancer."

"I'll be over in a second," Stoner said, and the green light went off.

"Michael, get her reprepped and draped for a radical. Ann, you scrub." He turned toward the nurse. "Dr. Meyer will be scrubbing, too."

Stoner looked at Meyer. "I'm sorry, Jon. Do you want to look at the frozen with me?"

"Yes," Meyer said, almost inaudibly, a feeling of nausea sweeping through his body.

They walked out of the operating room as everyone shifted gears. The little show was over and the big one was about to begin. Most of the people in the O.R. had been through it hundreds of times. For them, this was nothing out of the ordinary. For Cynthia and for Meyer, it was disaster.

Dr. Paley had intubated Cynthia and was taping the endotracheal tube in place. Michael Benedict was at the sink again, rescrubbing. For him, this would be boring. What the hell was going on? Whoever heard of two staff men scrubbing on a simple operation like a modified radical mastectomy? If Meyer didn't scrub, then he, Benedict, would have been able to first-assist or perhaps even do the case. With Meyer there, he would hold retractors for two or three hours. There were better things to do at his stage of training, he thought. Ann scrubbed quietly next to him. She'd only seen four, but she hated mastectomies.

Stoner and Meyer walked down the hall and into the common room that was part operating suite and part Department of Pathology. Jud Nadi was sitting by the microscope.

"Here, look for yourself," he said.

Ted looked first. "No doubt about it," he mumbled. Then Meyer looked. There were thousands of dark blue-stained cells without much of an organized pattern to them. They were all different sizes and shapes, dividing and growing wildly. The cells were out of control and there was no question: Cynthia had breast cancer.

Meyer didn't say much as he went back into the operating suite. He was overwhelmed with emotion and he felt sick inside. How could this happen? He had been so sure that it was benign. What could he possibly say to her, now? How would she ever be able to tolerate this?

"Do you really want to do this, Ted?" he asked as they walked down the long corridor.

"Of course," Ted answered. "It's what she needs and what she's agreed to have done."

Stoner looked at Meyer. "If I were you, Jon, I wouldn't scrub. You're obviously too involved and that's going to affect your judgment."

"What judgment? You're going to make all the judgments. I promised I would scrub and I will. I'm going to be a pair of hands that cares."

When they got to the sinks, Michael Benedict and Ann had just finished. "It's too bad," Michael said. "She's really a beautiful girl."

"Go ahead in," Stoner said, "and drape her widely."

Meyer and Stoner scrubbed for only a few minutes, but to Meyer it seemed like forever. As they walked into the operating room, the whole process of gowning and gloving was repeated.

Stoner and Benedict took positions on the right side of the table with Meyer, Ann and the scrub nurse opposite them. The exposed field was essentially the entire right chest.

Meyer had always been able to hide the patient before. But today, no matter how well she was covered, he knew it was Cynthia and there was no way that he could forget.

"She's lucky," Ted said. "With a breast this size, we'll be able to do an excellent cancer operation and she won't require a skin graft. Give me the marking pencil, please." And Stoner proceeded carefully to draw out the elliptical incision lines.

"Knife," he said. "And give me a fresh blade every time I ask for the knife again."

"Yes, Doctor."

As Stoner made the initial incision and blood oozed from the wound, Meyer realized that Cynthia would never be the same. It was irreversible. He felt empty and helpless.

Controlling the bleeding with the electrocautery, Stoner developed flaps that reached to the upper abdomen below, to the sternum on Meyer's side, to the large muscle—the latissimus dorsi—on his side and up to the clavicle on top. The operative field was extremely large.

Once the flaps were finished, the tedious work of the axillary dissection began. Stoner carefully weasled along the axillary vein, taking extreme care not to injure it. Snapping, cutting and then stopping to tie; a hundred tiny vessels, one by one, were ligated in this fashion.

When the dissection of the axilla was finally completed, the tension, which had gradually built up, eased; but the most gruesome part of the operation was to follow.

Meyer applied steady downward traction with the contents of the axilla, which he now held in his hand. This made it simple for Stoner to cut through the fascial plane that connected the breast to the chest wall muscles. Any bleeding vessels that previously supplied the breast were snapped with a clamp and then either tied or cauterized.

They continued to work their way down and then that inevitable moment came, a final cut by Stoner.

A flood of nausea hit Meyer. He fought the feeling to vomit as he handed the specimen to the scrub nurse and she put it into a metal dish.

Cynthia's breast was no longer part of her body.

For Meyer, it was the most horrible sight he had ever seen. For Ann, it was something she was going to have to learn to deal with. For everyone else, it was routine.

Stoner irrigated the wound with saline, sutured two suction catheters in place to prevent fluid accumulation and began to close.

"Why don't you drop out, now, Jon? We can finish."

Meyer didn't hear him.

"Jon," he said again, "why don't you drop out?"
"Oh, okay."

His gown and gloves off, Meyer sat on a stool in the corner of the room, unable to leave.

Benedict came to Meyer's side of the table and he and Stoner closed Cynthia's chest.

When they were through, Meyer looked at the result. It was a beautiful surgical triumph. It would heal nicely. But God, it was horrible!

The wound was bandaged just as Dr. Paley extubated Cynthia.

"It's all over, dear," Paley said. "Your operation is through."

He suctioned her mouth to remove any secretions.

"Wake up, Cynthia. Wake up, dear."

Cynthia was moaning as she came out of the anesthesia.

Ted leaned over. "It's all done; your operation is over."

Cynthia was only minimally awake. She said nothing and she was told nothing. She was transferred to a litter and wheeled down the corridor.

In the recovery room, the nursing team quickly took over her care.

She was becoming more alert and she somehow sensed that she'd been asleep for hours rather than minutes. She knew what had happened.

"My breast," she said, "my breast." She began to whimper.

Ted leaned over. "Cynthia," he said, "you had cancer. We had to do the big operation."

She screamed.

It was a tragic scene. It had happened before in this recovery room, but still, no one knew what to do.

Stoner ordered a sedative. Meyer went to her side and took her hand.

"It's me, Jon. You're going to be all right."

She continued to cry. As he tried to calm her, she looked at him and screamed, "Go away, go away. I hate you!"

She pushed his hand away and continued to moan.

The sedative finally took effect, she became calm and fell artificially asleep.

Meyer went down the corridor from the recovery room to the doctors' dressing room. He walked into the toilet and vomited his breakfast.

16

Meyer closed the door to Susan's office, turned left and walked down the corridor. As he waited for the elevator he looked at his watch. It was just past 1:00 P.M. He wondered how Cynthia was doing. Realizing that the X-Ray Department was on the same subbasement floor as the operating suite, he decided to continue down the corridor. When he neared the pressure-sensitive mats outside the recovery room, his pace slowed; he wished he were weightless as he stepped on the corrugated rubber sensor and the doors swung open.

The huge brightly lit room had organized space that allowed for at least forty beds. He headed diagonally across the room, around beds, past the central nursing station, toward Cynthia.

The door on the other side of the recovery room, coming from the operating suite, swung open and another patient was hurriedly wheeled in. Nurses in green scrub suits quickly surrounded the bed and wired the patient to a variety of electronic monitors, then hooked him to a suction apparatus and oxygen, completing the transfer in near record time.

As he approached, Meyer saw Cynthia's sleeping face

and was greatly relieved; there would be no scene. He picked up the chart at the foot of her bed and studied it; the straight lines reflected her stable condition. There was a bit of adhesive stuck on her cheek from where the endotracheal tube had been taped in place; he wanted to wipe it off, but he didn't. He could still see the slightly reddened outline around her mouth caused by the tight compression of the oxygen mask earlier in the morning. Although she hadn't lost much blood, she was quite pale. He stared as she slept and he marveled at her. She was still so beautiful.

He reached out and caught the arm of the nurse at the next bed, gently guiding her away. "I don't want her to wake up," he said softly, glancing back at Cynthia. "How's she doing?"

The nurse smiled at Meyer, somehow sensing that this was more than just a doctor's routine postoperative visit. "She's doing fine." Then she reeled off Cynthia's blood pressure, pulse and respiration.

"Has she been awake at all?"

"Once or twice since she got here, but not for long. She's very upset," she added, "but they all are."

Cynthia lay very still, listening to them whisper. She watched Meyer through her slightly opened eyes. Then she closed them tightly and continued to pretend she was asleep. She didn't want to see Jon Meyer ever again. He had helped them destroy her. She had cancer and she was going to die.

Why had they bothered to tear her apart, to rip off her breast? Her hand trembled and she hoped he wouldn't see it.

Meyer went back to his office, called Paul Cutler and

made a date with him for dinner. He put his feet up on his desk and stared out the window. He felt weary, heavy with thoughts; he didn't even know where to begin. How was she going to handle this? And what about him, what role was he going to play? What role would she let him play? How was she going to react to him when she'd awakened from the anesthesia and was fully rational again?

He drank coffee as he thought out all the possible questions; then he played through possible solutions. But there were just too many questions and not enough facts even to begin to construct any real answers. He was wasting his time.

He got up and headed for the surgical clinic. He examined two patients with the residents and then cornered Susan, asking her all the same unanswerable questions he'd asked her earlier that morning. After another soothing conversation with her, he still felt dissatisfied. He saw Anna Weber, the psychiatrist for the breast clinic, and walked over to her.

"I've got a real problem. Have you got a minute?" He led her into one of the empty rooms and closed the door.

"For you, Jon, I always have time," she said warmly.

Anna was someone Meyer trusted. In her late forties, tall, she had bits of premature gray scattered through her brown hair. Somewhat overweight, she seemed motherly.

He put the story together as coherently and succinctly as he could.

She listened intently and then looked at Meyer, asking softly, "Who is it you want me to treat, Cynthia or you . . . or both of you?"

Meyer smiled. "Don't be funny, Anna. I want you to see Cynthia as soon as possible."

"I wasn't being funny. May I speak openly?"

"Of course."

"I've known you for a long time, Jon. In some ways, I feel you are a troubled man. I've often thought of you as a highly accomplished but only partly developed person. A part of you is an outstanding teacher, researcher, innovator, clinician . . . let's just say a superb doctor. The other part seems a rather empty man who is uncertain about love. I'm sure that you would benefit from psychotherapy."

Taken off guard by her directness, Meyer stared at her, trying to find something to say. "I'm not afraid of love."

"Of course you're not afraid. You love this hospital and your work, your students, your patients. I'm talking about a special person. I'm talking about being able to love one person, a woman."

"I don't want to talk about me. I want to talk about Cynthia."

"I understand that, but I can't talk about her without talking about you. You have an involvement at this point that simply doesn't allow for the complete dissociation of the two of you. Her problem is separate from yours and, ultimately, she can be treated separately, but right now you're involved and things need to be sorted out."

"Will you see her?"

"First of all, she's not even your patient. I can't see her on just your say-so. You'll have to get in touch with Stoner and get his permission."

"I'm sure it'll be okay with him."

"Fine," Anna said. "Call me at home tonight and if

Stoner says it's all right, I'll stop by and see her tomorrow."

Meyer thanked her and left the clinic. He wandered about the hospital and finally took the elevator to 6-North. He stopped at the nursing station, went into the small room behind it and poured himself a cup of coffee.

Joan, one of the nurses on the ward who had been playfully flirtatious with Meyer for several years, was at a small table looking over one of the patient's charts. She looked up. "I'm sorry to hear about your friend."

So the word was out, Meyer thought, and everyone knew. This would become a major piece of hospital gossip, the first he'd ever been involved in; but he was too upset to care.

"It's really too bad," Joan said. "She was a beautiful girl."

"She still is," Meyer added quickly.

Joan smiled.

"Have you met her?" Meyer asked.

"Yes, when she first came in."

"What do you think?"

"I think she's in trouble. She's not going to tolerate this procedure very well."

"Why do you say that?"

"A woman can tell." Joan hesitated. "Your lady wore too much of her personality on her chest. Now, half of it's gone."

Meyer shook his head. "You didn't get to know her. There's much more to her."

"I'm sure there is. But regardless of what you think of her, the rest of the world has probably always treated her as just a pretty girl."

"Is she back yet?"

"Yes, about half an hour ago."

Meyer finished his coffee and walked down the hall to room 617.

He bumped into Ted Stoner, who was just coming out of Cynthia's room.

"She's doing great," Stoner said. "Everything's stable. She's afebrile. There's virtually no blood loss out of the Hemovacs and she looks good."

Meyer motioned for Stoner to follow him and they moved about ten feet down the corridor and away from Cynthia's room.

"Ted, she may look good on paper, but I'm afraid she may be destroyed by this. This is going to be an incredible blow to her self-image."

"Jon, she's fine. You're taking this much too seriously. Give her some time and she'll get over it. No woman likes to lose a breast."

"This is no ordinary woman. I know her. She's exceptionally wrapped up in her body. She's going to have a hard time."

"She's depressed like any other woman after a mastectomy. What the hell do you think she's supposed to feel . . . happy?"

"Ted, all I'm saying is . . ."

"Listen, Jon, you're too involved in this goddamn case. You've lost all your objectivity. You can't help her by thinking like this."

"All I want to do, Ted, is to ask your permission to let Anna Weber see her. She's had a lot of experience with mastectomy patients and I think it could be helpful."

"I think it's a goddamn waste of time and, besides, I thought you were going to stay out of this case."

"This is all I'm going to ask; you have my word."

"All right," Stoner said, "but that's it. Keep out of the case from now on. You're overreacting."

Meyer walked into 617. Cynthia was lying on the bed staring at the ceiling. She felt foggy from the anesthesia. And she was still numbed by the fear that had engulfed her the moment she'd awakened from the operation.

"Hi," Meyer said. She didn't answer. He pulled up a chair and sat down next to her. "How are you?"

"Dr. Stoner says I'm fine." The words fell out of her mouth. She didn't look at him.

"How do you feel?"

"How would you feel?" She wanted to yell at him. "I hurt."

"I know." He reached over to wipe her forehead, but with what seemed an enormous effort by her, she turned away from him.

"How do you feel inside?" he asked softly.

"Why don't you just leave me alone!"

Meyer smiled, weakly. "I'm sorry . . . I just want to help you."

Suddenly she began to cry, and then to sob, the tears running uncontrollably down her face. Her right arm was wrapped in an Ace bandage to prevent swelling and it rested on three pillows. Her left arm was attached to a board with clear plastic tubing carrying glucose and water through the needle in the back of her left hand. She was helpless as the tears ran off the side of her face and onto the pillow.

Jon grabbed a tissue from the bedside table and began to wipe her face. He felt tears welling up inside him. He wanted to cry with her, but he couldn't.

"It's a terrible thing, Cynthia. But you're a strong girl. You'll get over it. It'll take some time, but you'll be one hundred per cent, and soon."

"I don't want to be *one hundred per cent*," she sobbed. "I want my body to be whole and it's never going to be that way again . . . never!"

"Let me help you."

Her head turned sharply as though someone had struck her. She looked right at him. "You said a long time ago that you'd help me. And look what you did. You abandoned me."

"I didn't abandon you. Whatever I did had nothing to do with this. I told you . . . I just didn't want to fall in love with you, not just yet. I was pushing you away. I was protecting myself."

"So why don't you just keep pushing?"

He brushed her hair away from her forehead. "I don't want to." He waited, trying to get her to focus on his face. He wanted her to see that he cared.

"I talked with Dr. Anna Weber, today. She's a psychiatrist and . . ."

Cynthia interrupted, "I don't need a damn psychiatrist. I'm not crazy. My body's been mutilated."

"Anna's dealt with hundreds of mastectomy patients. She can help you to feel better."

"Don't you understand? No one can help me. My breast is gone. You can't put it back. I'll never be the same.

Never!" Never was a lot longer than she may have had, anyway, and she didn't want to think about that.

"But your femininity, your womanliness . . . it's all still there. You're exactly the same woman you ever were." He had to convince her to see Anna. "Dr. Stoner wants you to see her. He thinks it's a good idea."

Cynthia didn't really answer him. She just glanced away in silence, seeming to fall back into a sleepless stupor. The emotional effort to confront Jon had been enormous and out of her control. She didn't have any strength left to say no.

Meyer met Paul Cutler in the back of a small restaurant at about 8:30.

Paul looked at his watch and then up at Meyer, who was late. "Attorneys eat on time, you know." He smiled.

Meyer, who rarely drank hard liquor, ordered Jack Daniels on the rocks. Then he brought Paul up to date.

Paul listened, sympathetically, and sipped his scotch. "It's a shame. What's this going to do to your relationship with her?"

"I don't know."

"Well, all I can say to you is what I've said a dozen times before, 'You just don't fuck your patients.'"

"She wasn't my patient, she was Ted Stoner's."

"Bullshit, Jon. She was your patient and you fell right into the trap."

"It could have happened to anyone."

"Right. Only this time, 'anyone' was you. I don't care who held the knife, she was essentially your patient and you're up to your ass in it. Now we've got to figure the best way out for you."

"What are you talking about?"

"Well, there may be some legal implications here. I really have to give it some thought, but she may have grounds for a suit. You may have abused the doctor-patient relationship. She could say that you used your power as a doctor to seduce her. Then you switched doctors on her in midstream. Both doctors had different ideas about how she should have been treated and all that may not have been communicated to her. She may say that, in the confusion, she never gave informed consent."

"Wait a minute," Meyer said. "This is crazy. First of all, she'd never do anything like that and, secondly, she asked me to go out first."

"Who was present when she asked you out?"

"No one."

"Of course, so it's your word against hers. Here she is"—and he began to orate as though he were in court—"a beautiful, and now deformed, woman, and you the big stud surgeon with all the power. You could very easily have taken advantage of her."

"Paul, don't be ridiculous. She's never going to accuse me of anything like that."

"You never know. I've been involved in cases a lot more outrageous than this one."

Jon sat back and sipped his Bourbon. "This all sounds crazy," he mumbled. He leaned forward. "As far as informed consent, Cynthia may have been overinformed. She knew everything."

"You may have told her everything, but that doesn't

mean she understood it all. And that's what informed consent is. The patient must understand all aspects of the procedure—all risks, all choices, all alternatives and so on."

"Cynthia's not going to cause any trouble. I'm sure of that."

"You were sure she didn't have cancer, too."

"That was different. Even if she did say any of what you're suggesting, she couldn't prove it."

"I agree," Paul said. "It would be very difficult to prove but that's not what I'm worried about. What concerns me is that any of these accusations might be very embarrassing to your career. Once you're accused of things like this, it doesn't matter whether you win or lose, you've got a black mark that takes a long time to erase."

Meyer shook his head. "I suppose you've got a point, but I don't think it's a very realistic worry. Cynthia and I were very close to being in love."

Paul sipped his scotch and looked up. "Your best chance of being murdered in this country, nowadays, is by someone who loves you. And how can you talk about love? You haven't even been going out with the girl for two weeks."

"Time doesn't mean anything. There was something that was just right about her."

"I'm not trying to put the relationship down, Jon. I liked Cynthia, very much. Maryann and I talked about her. If there was ever anyone who seemed spontaneously and almost magnetically right for you, it was Cynthia. I'm just playing an intellectual game. You're my best friend and I care about you. I don't want you to get hurt, if, by some chance, this becomes a vindictive mess."

"That just won't happen, and if it did there'd be nothing I could do about it anyway!"

"Let me give you some advice, although I'm not trying to tell you what you should do. I realize it's a complex personal and medical problem. But the best thing legally—I repeat, legally—would be for you to stay her friend. Make sure her medical treatment is perfect and, as much as possible, document everything. In other words, protect yourself. . . . But don't make love to her anymore!"

By the time they left the restaurant, they both had had quite a lot to drink. Meyer felt a little confounded by Paul's professional advice, but he also felt relieved after having spent some time with his best friend.

But in spite of his mental and physical exhaustion, Meyer did not sleep well again that night.

On Friday morning, Meyer went to the hospital, made rounds and purposely did not visit Cynthia. He gathered his work together, settled in his office and waited for Anna Weber's phone call.

It was just after 11:30 when she rapped on his door and poked her round gentle face through the opening. "Can I come in?"

"Of course," Meyer said as he stood up and pulled a chair close to his desk. "Coffee?"

She nodded. "Black, thanks."

Meyer nervously went into the outer office and returned with the whole pot and a fresh cup. Anna looked at him, drank some coffee and then, with both hands, nestled the cup on her lap. "I saw Cynthia this morning."

Meyer stared back.

"She's not very talkative and she didn't really want to see me. But from all that you've told me and the little I got from her and the record, I can tell you that she's a very complicated young woman. And very beautiful, too." Anna sipped her coffee, than leaned forward and put the cup on the table. "Now, if she does agree to work with me, and she hasn't yet, then I can't be running to you every day and telling you all her personal secrets."

Meyer nodded.

"You're not even her doctor. Essentially, you're only her friend and if she and I are ever to build a relationship, it'll have to be built on trust. She must know that her hidden secrets and her deep feelings are safe with me."

"I understand."

"Good. Now, I told her that I'd be talking to you today. If you're going to continue to help her, there are things you'll need to know. But I've promised her that in the future I won't be confiding in you and she won't be able to talk to you through me."

Meyer picked up his coffee and sat back to listen.

"First of all, let's talk about the acute problems. She's a young, beautiful, single woman and she's lost a breast. For a variety of complicated reasons, she's tended to be somewhat narcissistic, very body- and, particularly, breast-oriented. The loss of a breast to someone like Cynthia is as devastating as the loss of a hand to someone like you and she's profoundly depressed over it. She's withdrawn and alone. She feels utter despair. Her reaction is as pronounced as any I've ever seen.

"She's afraid no male will ever be sexually attracted to her. She feels deformed, mutilated. . . . She feels raped."

Meyer said nothing.

"There are a number of nonphysical, nonsexual aspects of her life in which she's never developed much self-confidence. And there are obvious reasons why these developments were curtailed—like the abrupt death of her mother and, unfortunately, the less than open relationship with her father. Basically, though, I find her quite competent and creative and I'm surprised at her own lack of self-esteem.

"Mentioning her mother brings up another problem and that's her fear of death. Her recollections of her mother's last year are probably all too vivid now. Maybe she's dwelling on death and, perhaps, the uselessness of her operation. What good did it do if all the future offers her is a premature and painful death."

"She's not going to die," Meyer said. "She has at least an eighty per cent chance of a five-year survival. Perhaps more. Let's see what the pathology shows."

Anna looked carefully at Meyer. "When you say eighty per cent survival, she's going to hear twenty per cent nonsurvival . . . twenty per cent death."

Meyer stared across the couch. For a second, Anna reminded him of his ex-wife, Nancy.

"So death and deformity, her loss of femininity and sexuality are her most real and valid worries. Then comes you, Jon. She thought she was in love with you and perhaps you with her. But all of a sudden you backed off. She wonders whether you knew she had cancer all along."

"Of course I didn't know that."

"I know that. But you're going to have to convince her. She doesn't trust you anymore. You told her the lump was benign. It turns out it was malignant. You acted like you might have loved her and then you pushed her away."

"I explained why."

"That's not enough, now. You're going to have to win her trust and respect all over again. She saw you as a great man, an accomplished man, like her father, and then, all of a sudden, the way you acted toward her was no different from the way her father acted toward her."

"The night before surgery, I thought we patched things up. I was certain we were back on the right track."

"Her surgery has changed everything. Wherever you were emotionally, the night before surgery, you're far from there now."

Meyer stood up and walked across the room. He looked out the window. Anna stood up and followed him.

"What should I do?" he asked.

"I can't answer that. I'm not a mind reader and I don't know how you feel. If you care about her as much as she cares about you, then by all means you should continue the relationship. If she ever needed you, she needs you now. She really has no one. If you don't care, then the sooner you get out of her life, the better."

Meyer spent most of the weekend in the hospital dividing his time between multiple visits to Cynthia, rounds, teaching any student he could find and unsuccessful attempts at writing a new paper.

Visiting Cynthia wasn't very satisfactory. She remained cold and aloof, and her anger at him, although it waivered, always seemed to be present. Meyer's own feelings were becoming progressively confused.

He tried to share her pain and to dilute her anxieties. But how could he? Her hurt was hers and no amount of talking seemed to ease it. His guilt, whether real or created, grew, and Cynthia was unable and unwilling to help defuse it.

Meyer sat in his office and talked on the telephone. He bounced the situation from Paul Cutler to Susan Heller and then back again. They were all in agreement: he hadn't caused the cancer, he hadn't operated on Cynthia and he wasn't her doctor anymore. There was no reason for him to feel guilty. All he had to do was to be her friend.

By Monday afternoon the pathology report was ready. Stoner and his small entourage of Michael Benedict and Ann Collins paraded into Cynthia's room.

"Not even a half inch in diameter," Stoner announced, as though he were personally responsible for its small size. "The cancer was a tiny one. The rest of the breast was clear, no other primaries. And all the nodes were negative, all twenty-two of them. I would say that we're looking at close to an eighty-five per cent cure rate." He smiled one of his rare, proud smiles.

"Let's take a look at the incision."

Summoning some courage, Cynthia stared at him. "Then why did I need it?"

"Need what?"

"Everything you did. Why did I need it?"

"You needed it because it was the right treatment."

"Why?"

"Because," he said as though he were talking to a fifth grader, "if we didn't do it, we wouldn't know any of these things. . . . If we didn't take the lymph nodes, we wouldn't know they were negative. . . . If we didn't take the whole breast, we wouldn't know there was nothing in the rest of it."

He moved closer to the bed. "Now, let's take a peek." He pulled the covers down and exposed Cynthia's upper body. "Can you slip your nightgown down?"

Cynthia struggled, trying to pull the strap over her arm.

Stoner impatiently stopped her. "Here, just pull the whole thing up over your head."

Ann came quickly around to the other side of the bed to try to help her.

Cynthia closed her eyes as Stoner pulled the tape away from her raw chest and removed the dressing.

"It looks terrific," he said. "It's healing very nicely. Let me see you put your arm up over your head."

Cynthia did as she was told.

"Look at that," Stoner exclaimed, "four days post-op and she's one hundred per cent. Very nice, young lady." He turned toward Michael Benedict. "I'll tell you, the transverse incision and leaving the pectoralis major, that's the answer."

Benedict nodded his head in agreement.

Cynthia kept her eyes closed and said nothing. She could feel the cool air on her chest, yet she felt hot. Her armpits were moist with perspiration.

"Ann," Stoner said, "pull out those Hemovacs when we're done with rounds."

Ann jotted down the order on her scut list as Stoner and Benedict turned and left the room, neither bothering to cover up Cynthia.

Ann sat on the edge of the bed and helped Cynthia pull

the nightgown back over her head. "I'll be back in a while to take these tubes out. They haven't drained anything for two days, so they can come out. It won't hurt."

Cynthia looked at Ann. "Thank you."

Ann scurried into the hall, catching up with Stoner and Benedict, who'd already begun their discussion of the next patient. She interrupted. "Do you want me to order a Reach to Recovery volunteer for Rogers?"

Stoner frowned. "No. She's got a full-time psychiatrist, she doesn't need another shoulder to cry on."

Susan Heller, who'd visited Cynthia the day after surgery, tried again on Monday and Tuesday. But Cynthia was still unreceptive to her.

"I don't think I've ever seen anyone in so much internal pain," she told Meyer. "I don't know why I can't get to her. Maybe it's my close relationship with you?"

On Wednesday, Stoner announced that Cynthia could go home the following day.

"Is your aunt going to come out here and take care of you?" Meyer asked.

"I don't know."

"Why not?"

"I never called her."

Meyer looked at her sad face.

"I don't want anyone around. I can take care of myself." And she broke into tears. "I'm *one hundred per cent*," and she lifted her arms above her head.

As she put them down, Meyer put his arms around her

and, for the first time since surgery, he hugged her. She gave up and she pulled him even closer.

"I want you to come home with me, tomorrow," Meyer whispered softly.

"What?"

"I care about you. I want to spend time with you and I want to get to know you again."

"Why?"

"Lots of reasons."

"Do you love me?"

"I don't know."

She was completely silent. "I need you to love me," she whispered.

"In my own way, I do love you," he said.

"What does that mean?"

"It means that I need some time to work out my feelings and that, in certain ways, I'm as troubled as you are right now."

He pushed her back a few inches and kissed her gently on the lips. She kissed him and she said she would come home with him.

Early in the afternoon, Ann Collins came into Cynthia's room. She removed Cynthia's partially eaten lunch and set a small tray down on the adjustable stand over the bed.

"You're going home tomorrow."

Cynthia nodded.

"I've got to take out half your stitches now."

Cynthia sat up slightly, closed her eyes, pulled her nightgown over her head and lay back against the pillows.

Ann opened her small suture removal pack and picked

up the scissors and forceps. She looked at Cynthia's chest: her perfect, full left breast moving up and down with the rhythm of her breathing.

On the right side, the horizontal incision was neat and symmetrical, with dozens of vertical plastic sutures looking like railroad ties holding the wound together.

Slowly and methodically, Ann began to remove every other suture. She lifted the rabbit ears of each stitch, cut just below the knot and pulled. If this procedure hurt, Cynthia didn't react to it.

"All done," and Ann started to pull down Cynthia's nightgown.

As Cynthia opened her eyes, she looked at Ann. Ann's eyes were moist.

"Forgive me," Ann said. "I can't seem to get used to this operation, particularly on someone our age."

"Don't ever get used to it." Cynthia began to cry. "Or you'll turn into someone like Stoner."

"I've got something for you," Ann finally said. "I'll go get it."

She returned in a few minutes with a plastic bag. "I got this from the Reach to Recovery volunteer. Dr. Stoner didn't think it was necessary. Anyway, this is the kit they give out. It's got all sorts of information about mastectomies—where you can buy a permanent prosthesis; stores that sell special clothes. It's got a rubber ball and a rope for exercise and a temporary prosthesis."

Cynthia stared at the little kit, hesitant to accept it, afraid to touch the soft, padded false breast.

Ann pulled everything out and laid it on the bed in front of Cynthia, picking up the prosthesis and holding it up to herself. "We can pin this into your bra when you leave." When she noticed the horrified expression on Cynthia's face, it was too late.

With precision and caution, Cynthia began placing all of the helpful items back into their plastic container. She took the prosthesis from Ann's hand and stuffed it back into the bag, handing it all back to Ann.

"I don't need this, thanks."

Ann stared at her wondering what she'd done wrong. Just a moment ago they'd seemed so close. "I'm sorry," she said softly.

Cynthia hadn't even thought about leaving the safety of the hospital where the doctors and nurses had seen everything and were horrified by nothing. In this place, she was just one of many. She wasn't a freak and she wasn't ready to leave.

She looked up at Ann. "I don't have a bra with me."

17

Ann knocked softly on the door, opened it and poked her head in. "Are you awake?"

Cynthia looked up. "Oh yes, they don't let you sleep around here. What time is it?"

"It's almost seven." Ann walked toward the bed. She was carrying a small paper bag. "I'm sorry I had to come by so early. I've got to scrub at seven-thirty and I've got to catch Dr. Benedict and make rounds with him before that." She handed the paper bag and a key to Cynthia. "I got it."

"Thank you." Cynthia stuffed the brown bag into the dresser drawer beside her bed. "Did you get the right one?"

"Yes, and I brought another one that might work even better . . . one without the wires. It won't irritate your right side as much, but you should try both of them and then decide. By the way, you have a very nice apartment. And I watered all the plants. They're doing fine."

Cynthia wanted to take Ann's hand in both her hands and thank her, but she could only mumble her appreciation. She just couldn't show Ann her feelings. She was afraid she'd start to cry again, and Ann had said that she didn't have much time now.

Ann smiled as she handed Cynthia a small piece of paper. "Here's my home phone number; if you need me or you want to talk or have lunch some Saturday, just give me a call."

At that moment Stoner walked into the room. He frowned at Ann. "Dr. Benedict has already begun rounds, *Dr. Collins.*"

Ann looked back at Cynthia. "Take care of yourself and good luck." She turned and left the room.

Stoner sat on the edge of Cynthia's bed, smiling warmly at her. She was Meyer's friend and perhaps she did deserve some special treatment.

"You've done marvelously. Now, when you go home, just go about your life as though you'd never been here. Did the nurses show you some exercises?"

Cynthia nodded.

"Good! Do them as they instructed and you won't have any problems. I wouldn't do anything heavy with the right arm for a month or so, but slowly keep increasing what you do with it. You still have half the sutures in and I wouldn't get the incision wet until they're removed. When did we do you?"

She remembered; why couldn't he? "A week ago," she said softly.

"I usually take the rest of the stitches out at about ten days, so that would be around Sunday. Why don't you come in on Monday?"

"Should they come out on Sunday?" she asked.

"Doesn't make a bit of difference. If you're going to see Jon, he could take them out on Sunday, but otherwise, it doesn't matter. Monday will be fine."

"No, I'll come in on Monday." She didn't want Jon to do it.

"Fine." He extended his right hand, and Cynthia took it. "Good-bye. Do you have any pain?" he added quickly.

"It's still a little sore."

He pulled out a prescription pad, scribbled on it and tore off the top sheet. "Take aspirin for regular pain. If it gets to be more than aspirin can handle, take these, one every four hours." And he handed her the prescription. "Do you need anything for sleep?"

"I don't think so."

He wrote another prescription. "Very mild sleeping pills. Just to take the edge off, in case you can't fall asleep." He smiled at her again. "All right then, I'll see you next Monday. Call if you have any problems in between now and then." He turned and hurried out, failing to give her an opportunity to ask any real questions.

She ate a little breakfast when it came and then she went into the bathroom. Very cautiously she washed what she could of her body; she combed her hair awkwardly with her left hand, afraid to use her right. And she winced a few times, anticipating pain that never occurred.

Walking over to the night table, she took out the brown paper bag. It looked like a lunch bag that could have contained a tuna sandwich and an apple. For a moment, she wished she were still a little girl and that her mother had given the bag to her to take to school. But she didn't want to think about her mother.

She knew no one was in the room, but she looked around anyway, to make certain. Then she opened the bag and removed the two bras. She examined them both very carefully, like two foreign objects, and selected the one she'd originally asked for with supporting wires. She stuffed the other one back into the drawer.

She opened the second drawer, pulled out the Reach to Recovery plastic bag and carefully withdrew the cloth form from it; reaching also for a blouse, she went back into the bathroom.

Before removing her robe, she turned the lights off. In the dark, she searched for the hook and hung her robe on the back of the door. Although it was very dark, she still turned away from the mirror. She hooked the bra around her waist and then spun it around. Leaning forward, she fit her left breast into the soft cloth of the bra, then straightened up, picked up the soft white prosthesis she'd left on the sink and stuffed it gently into the crinkled right side. She quickly found her blouse, slipped it on and buttoned it.

Switching on the light, she turned and faced the mirror. She was appalled. The right breast was much smaller than the left one and as she moved her arm the bra and prosthesis rode up, the wire rubbing and hurting the tender flesh beneath it. The prosthesis just wasn't big enough or heavy enough. Disgusted, she sat down on the closed toilet seat, unable even to cry.

Finally, with some determination, she went back into the room and got the other, softer bra out of the top drawer. She went through the whole procedure again: turning off the light, bending over, stuffing her left breast into the cup, inserting the prosthesis in place and, this time, pushing a wad of facial tissue behind it. The lighter smaller bra fit better. When she was through and was able to look, she decided it didn't look as bad as before.

When she was fully clothed, she studied herself again in the mirror. Fidgeting, she tried to adjust both "breasts." She put her sweater on over the blouse but the lopsidedness seemed more obvious and she took it off.

She tried on her jacket and it seemed less noticeable. Back in the room, she sat in a chair for a while and tried to stop thinking about the way she looked. But she was certain that everyone was going to be able to tell and she wanted to run and hide.

Leaving the hospital seemed an even more humiliating experience. The nurses made her ride to the front door in a wheel chair, a hospital rule, making it apparent that she was a patient. And more painful than that, in spite of all her effort, it was obvious what she'd had done. She knew that all anyone had to do was to look at her.

She folded her arms across her chest as she rode to the front door, and she never looked up.

Meyer drove slowly up the winding hill. He negotiated the last curve and they were home.

Cynthia stared out the window as he came around to help her out of the old Porsche.

He carried her small overnight case directly into the bedroom and she followed him.

"This was stupid, I really should have gone home first. I need my things."

"I'll go for you this afternoon or we can go together, or we can go tomorrow. We'll get you what you need." He wanted to please her, to do something to make her just a little happier.

"I want to change and I have nothing to change into."

"Look through my drawers. You'll find something."

"Okay," she said reticently.

He didn't appear to be leaving the room and she looked crossly at him. "I'm going to change now."

"So what?"

"I don't want you to see me."

"I've seen you before."

"You may have seen me in the operating room, but that was different. You haven't seen me like this. *I* haven't even looked."

"You're going to have to let me look at you someday."

"Someday, Jon, but not now." And she began to cry.

Jon moved closer to her and put his arms around her, but she moved away.

"Please, Jon, leave me alone awhile!"

"All right," and he walked out of the bedroom. It was going to be tough.

She unpacked the few things she had and began looking through Meyer's drawers and closets for something to wear. She settled for a large blue-gray work shirt.

Taking off her clothes, except for her bra and panties, she quickly slipped into the shirt. She rolled up the thirty-seven-inch sleeves and buttoned the front, leaving only the highest button open. The shirt was large and it came down to her lower thighs, but more than that, it was baggy and what she could see of herself beneath the shirt looked quite normal.

She didn't feel completely comfortable, though, and she

continued to look for something to cover her legs with. She finally settled for a pair of sweat pants with an elastic waist, but they were much too long and although they covered her completely, she felt foolish. She pulled them off and threw them on the bed. She continued searching fruitlessly. Then she grabbed the sweat pants off the bed, took them into the bathroom and angrily cut seven or eight inches off the bottom of each leg. She tried them on again and, although they still fit poorly, they looked better.

Jon finally knocked and poked his head through the doorway. "Hi, I like your outfit." He smiled. "Do you want some lunch?"

She shook her head. "No, thanks."

"Do you want to come out on the deck?"

"In a while . . . I just want to be alone for now."

Meyer made lunch, put some music on the tape player and sat on the sun deck, by himself, for about two hours.

He didn't even know whether she had any friends. He'd been too caught up with the relationship, too busy with himself even to bother to ask. It was so typical of him, he thought, not to be interested in the mundane aspects of someone else's life. Nancy used to complain about that trait in him.

The tape ended just as Cynthia came out onto the deck.

Meyer went in, turned off the stereo and spent the rest of the afternoon, quietly, with Cynthia.

This was her first day up and around and she was very tired but somehow she gathered enough strength in the evening to go with Jon to her apartment and bring back a suitcase full of clothes.

After he'd helped her unpack, she looked at him. "I'm not sure if I can sleep in the same bed with you."

Meyer looked at her quizzically. "What?"

"I said, I'm not sure that we should sleep together in the same bed."

"Now why would you say something like that?"

"I don't feel right here. I'm just not comfortable."

"How could you not feel comfortable with me? We've spent lots of time together in this bed."

"Those nights were different . . ."

Meyer moved in front of her. He reached out, put his hands on her shoulders and pulled her close to him. "Cynthia, if I look at your body, I'm not going to be shocked by what I see. I mean, I've done hundreds of mastectomies. I know what they look like. I was there when yours was done. I know exactly what you look like and it won't affect me."

"I'm not talking about being turned on or off," she whispered. "I'm talking about being with you, caring about you. Are you just going to hurt me, again?"

Meyer didn't answer.

"Feeling comfortable has to do with how I feel about my body and how you feel about it. And it has to do with how we feel about each other as people."

"I think we feel good about each other."

"If I ever needed anyone to care about me, to love me, I need you now, Jon."

He held her tightly. He wanted her to feel wanted.

She pulled him even closer to her. "I've put my hand there and felt. It itches and I want to scratch but there's nothing there but the tiny ends of the stitches. There's absolutely nothing there! And it horrifies me. Can you understand that? Every time I think about it, it scares the hell out of me. It'll never be the same."

"There's nothing to be scared about," Jon said. "The worst is over. You've made it through the operation, you can only get better now."

"The worst is just beginning," she said softly. "I have to face the rest of my life like this."

Cynthia went into her bathroom and changed into her nightgown but kept on her bra and prosthesis.

Meyer, who started to undress when she returned, suddenly felt self-conscious changing in front of her. She'd turned away and was purposely not looking at him. He went into his bathroom and, for the first time in at least ten years, he put on a pair of pajama bottoms. He crawled into bed and kissed her. She responded, minimally, and it was over. She moved as far away as possible and they went to sleep.

18

Jon got up early on Sunday. He brought the newspaper into the bedroom and, quietly turning the pages, read until Cynthia woke up. He wanted to take her out to brunch, but she declined. By eleven he was getting fidgety. Remembering, he snapped his fingers. "You know what I've got to do?"

"What?"

"I've got to get your car."

He picked up the phone and called Paul Cutler, who agreed to shuttle him to the hospital, but not until late in the afternoon.

"Do you mind if I go out and play some basketball?" he asked Cynthia. "I need a couple of hours of exercise."

"Of course not," she answered, relieved.

And Meyer headed to the park, making it there by noon. On occasional Sundays, for years, he'd been playing ball with an ever-changing group of men. He played particularly well in today's pick-up game before going off to run a few miles. Whatever other exercise he liked doing, Meyer was always drawn back to the solitude of running.

It was hard for him to be with someone who didn't seem to want him around, someone who almost pushed him away. He knew things would get better as soon as she began to accept him and to trust him again. He was certain of it. All they needed to do was to make love.

As he jogged around the field, a dog ran in front of him. He was so deep in thought, he almost tripped over him.

He needed to show her that he would be just as turned on now as he had been when she'd had two breasts. He needed to show her that the loss of a breast wasn't the end: it didn't have to be equated with the loss of her femininity or her sexuality. She needed to let go, to relax, to turn on. And when that happened, it should certainly be with him.

Suddenly he thought, What if he failed?

That was stupid, he corrected himself. He cared about her and everything would be fine in bed.

But what if she got turned on and he couldn't? What if he couldn't get excited? No, that was ridiculous. There was no way this was going to affect him sexually.

He caught up with the shaggy dog who'd tried to trip him earlier and raced him across the field.

He told Paul about his fears as they drove to the hospital to pick up Cynthia's car.

"Imagine that," Paul said, "Jon Meyer, supersurgeon and stud, afraid that he can't get an erection." He smiled knowingly at Meyer. "It'll never happen."

Meyer drove Cynthia to the hospital at about 2:30 on Monday. He took her to Stoner's office and then went to the ward to say good-bye to Mr. Baum, who'd proven he was tougher than cancer or technical errors.

Stoner removed the last of Cynthia's stitches. "That didn't hurt, did it?"

"No."

"The wound looks excellent. Sit up a minute."

She did as she was told and he had her move her arms in a variety of positions.

"Superb result. It just couldn't be better." He smiled broadly. "Have you been doing your exercises?"

She shook her head, no.

"Well, it's certainly time for you to start, although it doesn't look like you really need them. Are you having any problems?"

Just at that moment the intercom buzzed.

"Excuse me," and he left her, naked from the waist up, sitting on the edge of the examining table.

"Sure, put him on," Stoner said into the phone. "Yes, Bill." He looked at his watch. "Great, I'll meet you on the first tee at five."

Cynthia had covered herself up with the paper sheet by the time Stoner hung up. "Where were we?" he asked.

"No, I don't have any problems," she said softly.

"Fine. I'll see you in two weeks then."

"I forgot to ask if I could take a bath or a shower," Cynthia said as she and Meyer were driving home.

"You can do either. In fact, you should, you're beginning to smell a little gamey." He laughed.

Cynthia didn't think it was funny.

"You can even drive your car," Jon said.

Cynthia went straight into the bathroom when they got home and began running the water for a long hot soak.

About fifteen minutes later, Meyer heard her screaming, "No! No! No!" He rushed into the bedroom.

She'd wrapped herself in a large bath towel and she was lying facedown on the bed, sobbing, trying to catch her breath.

Meyer put his hands on her shoulders, but she began crying hysterically and he couldn't calm her.

He sat there, at first, saying, "It's all right," but soon saying nothing.

Finally she quieted down and, without turning over, she sobbed, "I looked at it."

Meyer leaned over and kissed the back of her neck.

"It's disgusting," she moaned. And her crying intensified again.

Meyer tried to put his arms around her, but she wouldn't let him. "It can't be that bad," he whispered.

"I wish I were dead," she sobbed.

With that, he forced his arms around her. She squirmed, but he was much too strong and she quickly gave up. Meyer was behind her and they were both facing the same direction, his right hand underneath her, holding her right hand, and his left arm around her waist. He pulled her as closely to him as he could and kissed the back of her neck and her exposed ear.

"It's awfully hard for me to say 'I love you' to anybody," he whispered. "When I was a kid, I spent most of my time in the streets fighting with other kids. There was a premium on being tough, not on loving. In medicine, with surgery, I'm still a street fighter.

"And in my personal life, I've found that it's safer not to love. The few times that I've loved wildly and passionately,

I've gotten kicked in the ass. I've discovered that the further away I stayed, the better off I was. Most women tried to change me, tried to make me love. When they found out that I couldn't, or wouldn't, they tried even harder. . . . There must be something terribly attractive about a man who refuses to return love." He kissed her on the back of her neck again. "But, I'm going to love you."

Meyer moved his left hand from her waist to her thigh and, when she didn't resist, he began to rub her through the towel.

"No, Jon," she moaned, but she didn't fight.

He slipped his hand under the towel. She wanted him to touch her.

"No, Jon, not now. Please, it's too light in here and it's too soon."

He continued to rub her, and slowly she began to undulate her hips, moving them back and forth.

He wanted her and he was excited and happy that he wanted her.

He rubbed and stroked and touched . . . faster and faster. She moved faster and moaned. He rolled her over onto her back and opened the towel to her waist. She held her arms tightly across her chest, clamping the towel to her.

He looked at her beautiful body and what he could see of it was perfect. He began to kiss her stomach and then the inside of her thighs. She continued to move her hips up and down, faster and faster. Finally, her whole body tightened in a massive spasm and she had an overwhelming orgasm.

She started to cry again as Meyer crawled up next to her

and put his head beside hers. He could taste the salt in her tears.

She sniffed a few times, then smiled at him. . . .

They held each other and then Meyer slipped off his clothes. He was still excited.

Cynthia looked at him. She got up from the bed, continuing to hold the towel to her body, and she headed for the bathroom. "Would you close the curtains, please? I'll be right back."

Meyer smiled to himself. He assumed he'd handled it well. He knew he was right. All it would take was some time and support.

When she came out of the bathroom, she was naked from the waist down. On top, she was wearing her bra, with the prosthesis in place, and a tight-fitting Mickey Mouse T-shirt over it. It was small and it ended above her navel.

She stood at the end of the bed; her hands on her hips, her breasts sticking out, the small neat triangle of pubic hair, her full hips completely exposed, her smooth muscular legs slightly spread apart.

"Do you like it?" she asked.

It was an incredibly exciting outfit and he became more excited just looking at her.

"You're magnificent," he said. "Just look at me, do you think I like it?"

She laughed, for the first time, and it was real.

She crawled into bed with him and they made love.

They spent the whole evening in bed. It seemed as though they were beginning to get to know one another again.

19

"*Right* . . . *Give me* a quart of skim milk and a regular, a pound of Fleischmann's margarine, the one in the little tubs, and two containers of low-fat cottage cheese. Now, I'll give you the fruits and vegetables. . . ."

Cynthia had been ordering the groceries from the local market because they delivered them to her. Every other day she made a meticulous list as she visually imagined herself going from department to department: from dairy to produce, from produce to meats, and on and on.

She'd decided, a few days after she'd arrived at Jon's home, that she would take care of as much of the household routine as possible over the telephone, allowing herself more time to cook and clean and to relax. She was going to take good care of herself, but more than that, she was going to take good care of Jon.

When she was through with her order, she went back into the bedroom and looked at herself in the full-length mirror. She looked good today and she smiled at herself. She had nice color in her face, she'd gotten her tan back in the last week and she'd been eating better. She was beginning to get back to her old self, she thought.

Grabbing her bag off the bed, she headed out to her car. It was a beautiful day. She considered putting the top down, but decided she didn't really have enough time. She had a lot to accomplish.

She drove down Sunset Boulevard into Beverly Hills, turning left on Rodeo Drive and riding slowly past the beautiful houses with their pampered lawns and gardens, across Santa Monica Boulevard and into the commercial district. She pulled into a parking lot and smiled at the attendant, who knew her by now.

She stopped for a moment in front of the shop, deciding no matter how much the outfit in the window cost, she was going to buy it. She knew Jon would like the bright red satin. She was disappointed when the shop lady pulled the robe off the mannequin revealing the low-cut gown with its spaghetti shoulder straps.

"I get cold shoulders at night," she apologized. "I need something that has sleeves."

This had become her favorite lingerie shop and she'd already bought a dozen of their briefest panties and three of their lacey garter belts. Today she wanted a few short nighties. She picked two with lace borders, high square necks, puffed sleeves and a satiny material that was smooth and sexy and couldn't be seen through.

"I haven't got time to try them on," she told the saleslady. "I'm in a hurry."

Jon seemed to like everything she'd gotten so far and she was certain he'd like these. She headed toward the beach.

She hadn't been home in weeks and today was a perfect day to pick up some of the clothes that were going to waste hanging in her closet.

As she entered the apartment, she noticed a terrible stench coming from the kitchen. She'd probably left some garbage in the wastebasket but she didn't feel like emptying it now.

She headed straight for the closet, pulling out dresses, shirts and snug pants. She packed them carefully in a suitcase she'd gotten down from the hall closet and started to leave. As she looked around for a last time, she noticed all her plants were limp and dying, or already dead. Most were brown and crisp-looking and some had a white mildew clinging to their leaves and stems. Resigned, she placed her suitcase in the front hall, went into the kitchen and filled the water bucket with cool water.

As she poured the now useless fluid into the hanging plants, it ran quickly through the dry soil and dripped onto the rug. She didn't seem to notice. She made three trips with the can back and forth from the kitchen to the living room and then into the bedroom. Finally, she gave up. Not bothering to dry the rug or to empty the garbage, she left, closing and locking the door carefully behind her.

As soon as she sat down in the car, she took a deep breath. The beach's cool fresh air was a relief compared with the stifling air of her apartment. She rested for a moment, she'd been going so fast for the past few hours. Then she started her car and drove back to Jon's. She had to be home in time to receive the grocery order.

It was still early afternoon and she felt like doing something. The house was clean, the food hadn't arrived yet and she'd already planned the menu for that evening. She thought for a second, then impulsively picked up the

SIDE EFFECTS

phone and dialed the Holmby Hills Country Club. "Would you page Alice Stern, please?" And she waited.

Meyer was surprised by Anna Weber's question. If anyone should know how Cynthia was doing, it should be Anna Weber. He smiled. "I thought we weren't going to talk about 'your' patient and 'my' friend."

"She isn't my patient any longer."

"What do you mean?"

"She came once after you took her home, and we had a very good talk. Then last week, she didn't show up so I called her. She said everything was fine, there were no problems at home, that she really didn't need me. I tried to convince her to continue seeing me. I told her I'd leave the same hour open again this week and she finally agreed, but she didn't come yesterday, either."

"I'm sorry, Anna. I didn't know that. She never mentioned it to me. After the first session with you, I asked her how it went. She said fine, and since then I've avoided the subject. She's doing so well at home. I naturally assumed she was continuing to see you."

Anna shook her head. "Well, she isn't. What do you mean when you say 'doing so well'?"

"We're doing fine, the relationship is going well. We don't fight and we have good talks. As soon as we made love, it seemed to clear the air and everything got better. Cynthia still won't show me the scar, she covers it whenever we make love and when she sleeps."

"That's natural," Anna said. "Most women take quite a while before they show the incision to their husband or lover. It takes them time to feel comfortable, naked, in front of anyone. After surgery, lots of women make love in the dark with a baggy shirt on for months, occasionally for years. A small percentage of women never feel comfortable again."

Meyer smiled. "Well, we're already ahead. We make love with light in the room. And Cynthia doesn't wear baggy shirts. She wears tight sexy shirts. Sometimes, she wears nylons." Meyer blushed. "She's always got something different on."

"Do you talk about the operation, what's happened to her, her feelings about all of this?"

"Not really. I tried three or four times, but she avoided answering or changed the subject. She doesn't bring it up and neither do I, now. She seems happiest that way."

Anna looked concerned. "Is she depressed at all?"

"I don't think so. She seems to be taking it better, to be better adjusted than just about any young woman that I've ever seen. It's almost . . ."

". . . as though it never happened." Anna took the words right out of his mouth.

He nodded. "Exactly."

"I'm surprised at you, Jon." Anna looked disappointed. "Right under your nose and you don't recognize it. If it happened to any woman in the clinic, you'd be among the first to notice it. You know the story of the second-year medical student who walks into a room, hears a heart murmur so loud and so obvious that he thinks it's the patient's breathing."

"What are you talking about?" Meyer asked, laughing.

"In your terms, Jon, you've missed the diagnosis. You're describing a woman and, for that matter, a man, yourself, who are dealing with a problem by denying its existence."

"I'm not denying anything. I'm dealing with it in what I think is the most effective way for Cynthia. I'm allowing her to heal slowly, to be happy."

"Do you think this ritualistic dressing up before lovemaking is a good adjustment?"

"I think it's her only choice at this point. When she gets more comfortable with her body, things will change."

"Do you think never talking about it, never admitting to herself that she's had a mastectomy, is healthy?"

"It's one way of handling the problem until the pain subsides."

"The pain will never get eased by itself. Somewhere along the line, she has to pay. When you were in high school and you lost a girl friend, what happened?"

"I got depressed."

"Yes! And you talked and talked to your friends and finally the pain went away. When we have a loss, Jon, when we lose the man or woman we love, or a part of our body, or our mother or father, we mourn the loss."

"I don't know how else to handle it," Meyer admitted. "This has all seemed so natural."

"Urge her to come back to see me again. Bring up the problem, talk about her feelings once in a while at home. Get her back out into the world. Start relating to people again as a couple."

Meyer nodded his agreement.

"She has my number, try to encourage her to call me."

Meyer was surprised when he saw the small two-tone brown Mercedes coupe parked in his spot in the driveway. He parked in the street and walked into the house. He found Cynthia sitting with another woman on the sun deck.

Cynthia smiled proudly and stood up when she saw him. "Hi, Jon. What are you doing home so early?"

"I thought I'd take you out to dinner tonight."

"That would be great." She stepped toward him, leaned forward and kissed him softly on the lips. "This is my good friend Alice Stern. Alice, this is Dr. Jon Meyer."

Alice looked up at Meyer and extended her hand. "So this is the mystery man. I'm very happy to meet you finally."

Meyer shook Alice's hand, then pulled up a chair and sat down next to her.

"I wasn't even sure you existed," Alice said coyly.

"I exist."

"You most certainly do." Alice looked at him admiringly. "I think Cynthia was right, you were worth waiting for."

Meyer smiled. "Thank you, but you can't tell just by looking."

"I've heard enough about you to be sure. Only a very special person could steal Cynthia away and make her miss the club championships."

"I didn't know she missed them."

"She did and she would have won this year. But even I might leave town, and my husband, for a few weeks in Acapulco with someone like you." Alice grinned cutely as Cynthia glanced quickly at Jon and then returned Alice's grin.

Meyer took a sip of Cynthia's juice, wondering what else

she'd been telling this lady. "How do you two know one another?"

"Hasn't Cynthia told you about me?" Alice feigned disapproval.

"She probably has," Jon said, "but I'll get the full story from you."

Alice smiled. "We've known one another for years, ever since Cynthia was a pretty little girl."

They chatted for a short while, Cynthia letting them get to know one another. Luckily, Jon had been to Acapulco, so when that subject came up again he handled it easily.

Alice looked at her watch. "Oh, it's late. I've got to get home and make believe I've played some role in creating dinner." She stood, told Meyer again how very pleased she was to meet him and how happy she was for them both.

Meyer could understand Cynthia's not wanting to tell this woman about her mastectomy and he could certainly excuse Cynthia's lie about three weeks in Mexico. She had to tell Alice that she'd been away, to explain why she hadn't been at the club playing tennis.

Cynthia returned from the front door, smiling. "Do you know what Alice said to me?"

Meyer looked up. "What?"

"She asked me why I was wearing a bra. I told her you said it was better for my body. And then she said, 'You look better in a bra.'"

Meyer wasn't certain whether Alice's remark made Cynthia happy or upset and he didn't know what to say.

Cynthia broke into a broad grin. "She couldn't even tell!"

Meyer smiled. "You do look wonderful. How about dinner out tonight? Did you mean it?"

Cynthia's grin disappeared and she hesitated. "Yes, I meant it."

Jon called his favorite French restaurant, went for a jog and showered. He put on his dark green three-piece suit, picked up the phone and dialed the hospital, informing them that he'd be out for the evening but that he could be reached with the beeper if they needed him.

Cynthia came into the living room. She'd done her hair and put on her make-up, but she hadn't gotten dressed yet. She stood in the middle of the room, tying the belt of her long terry-cloth robe.

"I just can't go," she said softly. "I just feel too tired." She didn't wait for a response. "I've been out most of the day running around. I feel rushed and . . . I really haven't been out at night yet." She looked at him, hoping he'd understand. "I'm really not up to it." Then she added quickly, "I have plenty of food here, I could make something."

Meyer took her in his arms. "It's all right. There are plenty of nights; we'll go out soon." He kissed her gently. "It's chilly tonight. Why don't I make a little fire? We'll drink some wine and we'll just relax and talk."

"I'd like that better," she said, feeling relieved.

They spent two hours in front of the fireplace. Jon wanted to bring up seeing Anna Weber again, but tonight just didn't seem like the right time to initiate that conversation.

"I liked your friend Alice. Why don't we have her and her husband over here someday."

"Oh, you'd like Michael Stern," Cynthia said. "He's the president of a record company."

"Why don't we ask them over here Sunday afternoon? We could cook some steaks outside."

Cynthia thought for a second, then seemed to be very enthusiastic about the idea.

Jon waited for just a moment. "How about the Hellers and Paul and Maryann?"

"Oh, sure."

Jon smiled. "We'll have a good time."

"I know we will," Cynthia said.

20

The barbecue was a success, everyone came and everyone had a good time. Jon's friends seemed to enjoy the Sterns, Jon was a fine host, making drinks and cooking the steaks. And Cynthia was an almost surprisingly perfect hostess.

No one mentioned Cynthia's operation. Jon had been sure that none of his friends would mention it, but just in case, he'd warned them not to.

Susan had wanted to say something positive and supportive when she and Cynthia had been alone, but Cynthia was so busy and doing so well that it seemed unnecessary. All Susan could really do was to admire Cynthia, as she watched her carrying on as though nothing had ever happened.

Meyer had also informed his friends about the trip to Acapulco and, although they would avoid the subject if it came up, they'd know how to handle it.

Everyone drank wine and talked, sitting outside and watching the sun go down. By nine o'clock, full of positive feelings about the day and the people, Meyer and Cynthia said good-bye to their friends. Even Meyer's fantasy day hadn't been this good. And Cynthia was elated.

Meyer put his arm around her as they walked into the

bedroom. "It was a perfect day and you made it that way."

"Thanks."

He turned her toward him and they kissed, at first softly, then harder, more passionately.

His hands slid down her back and he held her by the buttocks; as they continued kissing, she began to move her hips slowly back and forth. She was making small moaning sounds as she began touching him; they both were highly aroused.

It was like the first time again. The cautious defensive shielding that had surrounded Cynthia since her release from the hospital was finally gone. She trusted him again, he could feel it.

They continued to kiss and touch as Meyer unzipped her jeans and pushed them down. She wore no underpants.

He wanted to be inside her, to be part of her body, to be as close to her as he could possibly be.

"Oh, Jon, make love to me," she whispered.

He stood and began taking off his clothes. He gently pushed her onto the bed and slid effortlessly into her. They began moving back and forth, faster and faster, wilder and wilder, violently.

As she rolled on top of him, Meyer's hands went from her buttocks to her back and then to her *breasts*. He wanted to touch her, to kiss her breast.

In a fraction of a second, he pushed up her T-shirt and her bra. The prosthesis fell onto the bed as he took her left breast into his mouth. He sucked violently on the erect nipple and simultaneously they both came, an overwhelming, powerful orgasm.

They stayed locked together, covered with sweat,

Cynthia collapsing on top of him. They continued gently kissing, warm loving kisses. It had been the best love-making they'd ever had.

They held onto each other, not moving. Then Cynthia rolled over onto her back. He held her hand and he felt good. Everything was going to be all right.

Suddenly Cynthia moved her free hand from her side to her stomach and then to her chest.

"Oh, my God! OH, MY GOD!" She began screaming. "What have you done?"

She pulled her other hand free and with both fists she began to hit him. Her arms were flailing wildly, beating his face and head and chest.

"You bastard! You bastard! I hate you!"

She was totally out of control.

Meyer grabbed both of her wrists in an attempt to protect himself and she began kicking at him. She was strong, almost more than he could handle. He threw his body on top of hers, pinning her down, trying to stop her blows.

"Get off me!" she screamed.

"Stop it!" Meyer yelled.

She wriggled partly free and brought her knee up sharply into his groin. It knocked the wind out of him and it angered him. Stunned, he pinned her shoulders to the bed with his knees.

"I hate you!" she screamed, and she spit in his face.

He slapped her and she began to cry, but she stopped fighting.

As Meyer slowly got up, she was crying hysterically. He pulled her T-shirt back down over her, covering her nakedness and her scarred chest.

He was trembling and out of breath. "I'm sorry," he said softly.

But she made no response.

"I did it because I felt so close to you." He pulled the blanket up to cover the lower half of her body.

She lay on the bed, staring at the ceiling, breathing heavily, not really crying anymore, not making any sound. Her eyes were glazed and there were tears welling up, spilling onto her cheeks.

Meyer kissed her forehead and begged her again to forgive him.

She said nothing.

He walked into the bathroom, wrapped a towel around the lower half of his body and stared into the mirror. He couldn't remember an experience more horrifying than this.

As he sat down on the edge of the bed, Cynthia continued to stare blankly at the ceiling. She made no response and she didn't acknowledge his presence. He sat with her for perhaps an hour, telling her again and again how sorry he was. Still, she said nothing.

He had no idea what to do to help her. Finally, he went to the phone in his study and called Anna Weber. He felt tremendously relieved when she answered.

"I'm not surprised," Anna said calmly, after he'd told her what had happened. "Something like this had to occur. Only I didn't expect it to be quite so violent."

"Why didn't you warn me, Anna?"

"I did. I told you she was using an inordinate amount of denial. Don't go thinking that if you hadn't pushed her bra off that everything would have been all right. Maybe it would have been fine tonight, but then some other episode in the near future would have triggered her. Something like this was bound to happen and, believe it or not, it's a step in the right direction. Tonight you've both finally begun to realize what's going on. It was a horrible experience that neither one of you will ever forget. What's important is that you can change directions now, and as painful as that may be, you've got a chance to help yourselves, to pursue a far more realistic course. Go see how she's doing and ask her if she wants to talk with me."

"Okay, hang on."

Cynthia was lying on the bed in the same position. He sat down next to her, picking up her hand and tenderly kissing it. "I just talked to Anna Weber. She said tonight was actually a good thing, a step in the right direction. . . . She wants to talk with you."

Cynthia said nothing.

"Would you like to talk to Anna?"

"No," she said quietly and began sobbing again.

"Let me tell her that you'll talk with her," he pleaded. "She cares about you."

Cynthia didn't say no again, and Meyer left the room.

"She's coming over in thirty minutes," he said softly when he returned.

"Not tonight," Cynthia mumbled.

"Anna's worried about you. She wouldn't wait until tomorrow."

Cynthia said nothing.

"She cares about you and she wants to help."

"I don't need any help."

"She just wants to speak with you."

Cynthia got up slowly. "Okay," she said softly. She went into the bathroom, washed her face, combed her hair, put on a bra and prosthesis and covered everything with a robe.

By the time she came into the living room, Meyer had made a pot of coffee and she sat down quietly and drank a cup. They didn't speak to one another. Anna Weber arrived a few minutes later.

"We're going to use your study, Jon," she said, and the two of them left.

Meyer sat in the living room. He put on some old Dylan music. He was uncertain about what had happened, how he felt, where all this was going. He had no answers.

The only thing he knew for sure was that it was already after midnight, he had a 7:30 case in the morning and he was a long way from going to sleep.

21

"*I've been arguing* with myself for over a year and I still don't know how I feel about being reconstructed." Susan Heller stared across Meyer's desk, waiting for his support. "I saw Phil Dolman, like you suggested. He wants to reconstruct me."

Meyer nodded. "I know."

"Why is it so important to me? I'm doing so well the way I am. I just don't know if I could go through with it."

"Well, let's talk about the purely physical aspects first." Jon was going to be a good, official friend to Susan. "There's no sign of recurrent cancer. The skin on your chest is supple and there's plenty to work with. So there's no medical or physical reason not to go ahead and I would anticipate a technically excellent result. But it's true, excellent surgical results are a far cry from what God gave you.

"If you have it done, you wouldn't have to wear an external prosthesis and your bra wouldn't ride up when you are physically active. You wouldn't have to worry about being asymmetrical. I don't know that you'd look any better in clothes, though. You look fine now.

"The only disadvantage is that you'd have to go through the process of having it done. You'd be in the hospital for a couple of days, but Phil told me he could do it under local. So it would be a relatively minor technical procedure."

"I'm not concerned about the inconvenience or the surgery. Why do I want it so much? That's what's bugging me. Why do I think I need it? I've seen reconstructed patients in the clinic." She shrugged her shoulders. "Some of them are nothing to brag about. Phil said I'd still have the scars from my original operations and if he makes nipples out of labial skin, they wouldn't look very real. . . ." She hesitated. "Louis married me without breasts and he never complains. Why do I think it's so important?"

Meyer smiled at her. "I can't answer that one for you, but I'm a good listener."

She smiled back. "Oh hell, Jon, I'm still shy when I'm naked in front of Louis. My chest is flatter than his! I feel funny when I look at myself in the mirror or when I walk across the room undressed." She held her hands to her chest. "I miss their bounce, their soft protection. I don't stand up straight anymore, I slouch. It's ridiculous, but I just want breasts!"

"Look, Susan, this is an emotional decision. I know you aren't worried about your femininity. I know you feel perfectly womanly and that you don't have to prove anything to the rest of the world. This is something that's for you and you don't have to justify it."

"If a plastic surgeon creates two artificial lumps on my chest and I don't like them, then what'll I do? I'm not sure that, psychologically, that wouldn't be a worse situation."

"The prostheses can always be removed."

"Then why should I go through all this in the first place?"

"Because it's not a lot to go through for something that you really seem to want. The odds are that you'll be delighted with the results and there's virtually no risk."

"Then why do so few women get reconstructed?"

"Dozens of reasons—they don't know about it; it's not offered to them; it's expensive; they've lived with a mastectomy for a few years and they don't want to go through the bother. . . ." He hesitated. "Most patients have one breast remaining and one breast is a lot more than none."

Susan nodded. "You're so right. The loss of my second breast was almost more devastating than the first. I was more equipped to handle the experience, but inside it really hurt. I never thought I'd date again. At least with one breast, I could always show them my good side."

She laughed and then sighed. She didn't mean to go around in circles. She knew all along that she was going to have the operation. She just needed to talk it through again, to reason it out for herself one more time.

"I know half a dozen young women who've been reconstructed during the last year," Meyer said. "Would you like to meet with one or two of them, ask them how they feel, take a look at the results?"

"That would be great!" Now, *that* was a good idea, Susan thought. She could sit down and talk with someone who'd been through it, ease her mind a little. After all, there were other women who also thought it was important to have some facsimile of breasts as a part of their bodies. She wasn't the only mad woman who missed her soft, rolling chest.

Meyer leaned forward and wrote himself a note. "I'll take care of it."

Susan smiled. "Thanks."

There was a pause in their conversation, both of them hesitating before bringing up the next topic. Susan looked around the room and then back at Meyer. "How's it going at home?"

"Not bad, I guess."

"Good. I've been wondering how you two were getting along."

"Cynthia's fine. She's very tolerant of me. She's not too irritable. She never really complains. She's just depressed." He frowned. "And I guess that's the way it's supposed to be, for now."

"Every woman handles it a little differently."

Jon nodded. "She sees Anna Weber almost every day. That seems to be her whole life. She doesn't want to go out anywhere else, not even to the movies. I don't know what the hell she does around the house the rest of the time."

"You've just got to be patient."

Jon leaned forward and rested his chin on his palms. "Do you know what we had a fight about the other night?" He didn't wait for her response. "She was still taking her birth-control pills and I blew up at her. Stoner should have told her to stop two months ago."

"Why didn't you ever tell her to stop?"

"I never thought of it. It was so obvious. Everybody knows you're not supposed to take birth-control pills after breast cancer. I assumed Cynthia was aware of it."

"Why did that make you so angry? She just didn't know."

"I couldn't believe she hadn't figured that out." Jon

looked down at his desk and paused. "No . . . that's not the reason. I should have taken more responsibility during the first month when we were making love every day. I didn't even think about contraception. I should have told her not to take the pill when she first came home from the hospital. She just wasn't taking good care of herself and it was my fault. I was stupid and it infuriated me."

"I hope you didn't scare her."

"I don't think so. I reassured her after I calmed down. I don't think a couple of months on low-dose oral contraceptives could really do much harm. I apologized and told her that I was just mad at myself for not mentioning it sooner."

Susan knew how to be a good friend to Jon, also. "It's not just your fault," she said. "You should kick Stoner in the ass for this too."

By the time Cynthia woke up, Jon had already been gone for hours. She couldn't remember the last time she'd gotten up before he'd left for the hospital.

Getting out of bed was the first dreaded move of the day: it meant going into the bathroom with all of its mirrors. Although she'd devised numerous ways to avoid looking at herself, whenever she caught a glimpse of what was left of her body, she would become obsessed, standing there, staring. Getting dressed was just another part of the day that had been designed to hurt her.

The only appointments she kept were with Dr. Weber. She saw her three times a week, and if there was a cancellation, like today, she'd take the extra session. What else did she have to do?

SIDE EFFECTS

She couldn't go back to work and she couldn't possibly go to the club. Everyone there probably knew about her, and if they hadn't heard, all they had to do was to look. She would never be the same again and she never wanted to see any of the people who'd known her before!

She dressed quickly, not bothering to put on any make-up. She pulled the covers up on her side of the bed, but she didn't bother making it. Avoiding the kitchen with the last few days of dirty dishes piled in the sink, she headed straight out to her car. She made certain the top was tightly closed and she slid shut both the windows even though it was beginning to be a warm day.

For the first ten minutes of the session, she didn't say a word other than mumbling "Hello" when she'd arrived. She really didn't have anything to say. Everything was the same today as it was yesterday and the day before, so why bother.

Anna sat quietly with her, waiting patiently before she finally spoke. "Is there anything you're thinking of that you'd like to talk about today?"

Cynthia shook her head. Her mind was blank. She really didn't want to talk.

"I'm here to listen to anything you want to say. . . . Anything, no matter how small or insignificant you might think it is, could be helpful." Anna wanted to encourage Cynthia, but she didn't want to pressure her.

Anna had asked about Jon during previous sessions, but Jon often became an excuse for Cynthia to avoid talking about herself. They'd talked about Cynthia's mother and father, and understanding her relationship with them would be a key to the long-term working out of many of

Cynthia's more chronic problems. But, for now, Cynthia needed to deal with the mastectomy, to admit to herself what had happened and then, ultimately, to others.

"I have nothing to say, nothing happened that would interest you."

She and Jon had had a fight the other night, she could talk about that. She hated herself for getting angry at Jon and she was afraid that, if she did it very often, he'd throw her out. Even Anna might get sick of her if she kept talking about her problems.

"You're here, Cynthia, to talk about yourself and your problems." Anna was reading her mind. "I want to hear whatever you are thinking. I want to know how you are feeling."

"Why don't you ask Jon?" Cynthia blurted out. She just didn't quite trust Anna yet.

"I don't discuss you with Jon, you know that."

Cynthia sat quietly for a few moments and then she apologized. "I'm sorry." She just didn't want Anna to know how bad things were, how miserable she was and she'd groped for an excuse. She wanted Anna to think that everything was all right, that everything was getting better. "It's not your fault that I don't have anything to say today."

"Cynthia, we have lots of work to do together. We have just begun. Say what is on your mind. Let me be the judge of how important or unimportant it is."

Cynthia nodded, but didn't say anything for a few more minutes. Suddenly, everything seemed important and she didn't know where to begin. Everything scared her. She didn't think Jon loved her and, if he did, she knew she was going to lose him. She didn't think her father loved her and she'd lost him before she'd had time to find out. She knew she loved her mother, but she never really got a chance to tell her. She never got a chance to comfort her or to take care of her when she was sick. And, anyway, where was her mother now when she needed her? She was so unhappy, so depressed. Everything was connected to everything else and she just didn't know what to say first.

"I didn't clean the house today, or yesterday, or the day before."

Anna waited.

"I don't seem to care anymore what I look like or how I live."

"What do you mean?"

"That it doesn't matter. I'll never be the same again and nobody cares, not even me."

"I care."

Cynthia looked away from Anna's open gentle face. "You can't . . ." Cynthia began to cry. "You can't help me."

22

Jon thought about it. It would do Cynthia a lot of good to visit Susan, to see how well she was doing. She could see and talk with a woman, a friend, who had lost both breasts and had now had them reconstructed. It might give Cynthia some perspective about her own problems. She needed to learn that these things happened, that other people suffered and came through all right. It didn't have to be as difficult as Cynthia was making it on herself. He had to keep encouraging her.

"I'm going back to the hospital tonight," he finally said.

Cynthia was taking a last sip of coffee and thinking about cleaning the kitchen. "Go ahead," she replied softly. "You've been at the hospital late all week, I guessed things are pretty busy for you."

"I'd like you to come with me."

Cynthia looked at him carefully. "Why?"

"I'm going back to visit Susie."

She shook her head. "I don't want to go, Jon."

"I know she'd be really happy to see you, to see us together."

"I can't go, it's not right."

"What does that mean?"

"I mean that I just can't go, not tonight."

"But she's not going to wait in the hospital until you decide to go. She had her operation yesterday and she's going home tomorrow. I know she'd like to see you."

"Jon, I can't go, not tonight." She just couldn't go! She didn't want to go to the hospital and she didn't want to see Susie and have to talk to her. Why couldn't he understand? "Why don't you go without me?"

"Because I want to go with you."

"Jon, I don't want to go!" She could feel the heat flush on her face. She was afraid he was going to make her go.

"Why can't you think of someone else for a change?" His voice was raised. "When are you going to stop dwelling on yourself?"

"I don't want to go to the hospital!" She stood up. Trying to calm herself, she began gathering the few dinner dishes that were still on the table. She stopped before going into the kitchen and looked directly at Jon.

"You tell Susie for me that I'm glad everything worked out and that I hope to visit her soon."

"All right, I won't go either." Meyer was resigned. "I saw her twice today. I just promised that I'd come back with you."

"You shouldn't have promised."

Making Cynthia feel guilty wasn't the right approach and Meyer knew it. "I didn't really promise. She asked for you and I told her that if you felt up to it I was sure that you'd like to come tonight. It made her smile. She likes you."

He reached out for Cynthia's hand but she pulled away. Silently berating herself, she went into the kitchen. Jon had made several requests lately, simple requests, but she had said no to all of them, each one seeming more impossible to her than the last. She was as frustrated with herself as he seemed to be. She was afraid of so many things and she just didn't want to test herself, not tonight.

Meyer sat at the dinner table, knowing that he'd tried to make her feel worse, hoping that she'd come and find out that it wasn't so difficult. How many more nights could the two of them sit here together without driving one another crazy? How many more evenings could they spend not talking about what was really bothering them or what was really important? How many more weekends could he spend isolated from his friends?

When she came back, he said he was sorry. "We'll visit Susan when she's back home and the stitches are out and everything is fine."

"Thanks for not making me go," she replied.

They went to bed early. Cynthia wore a heavy baggy shirt with a bra and prosthesis underneath. She closed the drapes completely and, with the lights off, the room was totally dark.

It had been more than a week since they'd made love and Meyer reached over for her. She didn't say no, and he continued.

He caressed her thighs and then slowly his hand went to her vagina. It was dry. He found her clitoris, but it didn't help. He pushed the covers down and he went to her with his mouth. But she pushed him away.

"Not tonight," she said and she reached over to the night-table drawer. She took some Vaseline and rubbed it onto her dry, and now chaffed, tender parts. She took more and applied it to Meyer's limp penis.

Meyer lay back, frustrated, sad, as she began to massage him. He thought about Susie and the hospital and his excitement and enthusiasm waned even further. He quickly purged his mind and began thinking sexual thoughts, fantasizing, remembering love-making with Cynthia before her surgery. His body started to come alive, but not completely.

Cynthia pulled him slightly toward her as she lay back. Knowing what that signal meant, Meyer rolled over on top of her. She took his partially hardened penis in one hand and inserted it in her artificially lubricated vagina. He pumped a number of times as she lay there, but he was still not fully erect. He pulled out, rolled over onto his back and reached over to his drawer. "Got to put something on," he mumbled.

He ripped the condom's tin foil open, pulling out the protective skin. He slipped it on and got back on top of her. His mind wandered and he started thinking about women he'd known before Cynthia, about undressing them, about fucking them. He got fully erect and he came.

When he was through, he threw the condom into the toilet. He got back into bed and quietly went to sleep.

23

Meyer apologized to the small group of students and walked out of the conference room. He had been intellectually ripping them apart. Starting the seminar passively, like a complacent has-been professor who'd been around the university for years, he'd given them all the right information but without the old reliable Meyer sparkle. Then, when one of the students had missed a relatively simple question, he'd turned on them, firing questions in rapid succession, interrupting their partial but often correct answers with additional questions, never validating any of their responses, making them feel like medical incompetents.

He felt badly as he walked down the corridor to his office. Why had he thrown a student out of the operating room yesterday, embarrassing him in front of everyone by sending him to the library when the student hadn't known a simple bit of anatomy?

Teaching just wasn't any fun today and it hadn't been for several weeks now. The medical detective games that Meyer was an expert at creating, that he had virtually developed into an art form, were now becoming a chore for him.

He walked angrily through his front office, without acknowledging Betty, into his own office and slammed the door.

He sat with his feet up on the desk for a while. Then, picking up the phone, he called Paul Cutler.

It was unusual for Meyer to leave the hospital complex for a meal, and it was even more unusual for him to initiate the invitation.

Meyer drove quickly into Beverly Hills, weaving from lane to lane, occupying his mind with the curves in the road.

He pulled into the Linden Street entrance of the Executive Life Building, wound his way up to the second-floor parking level and, like most Porsche owners, asked the attendant if he could park the car himself.

He got off the elevator on the eighth floor, walked through the already opened heavy oak doors and informed the receptionist that he'd arrived.

Paul Cutler, attired in a light brown three-piece suit, without the jacket on, came out to greet him. "It's about time you got your ass over here." Paul embraced Meyer. "Come on in, I want to show you my new desk."

Paul led the way down the familiar corridor into his elegant corner office. "Look at that!" he exclaimed. "There's a guy in Santa Monica who makes these to order . . . in his garage. This one took four months."

Meyer ran his hand across the desk top, feeling and smelling the oils that had been painstakingly rubbed into it. "It's beautiful," he said.

"Thanks. Twenty-six hundred bucks and that's because he's my friend. Do you want some coffee?"

"No," Meyer replied. "Come on, let's go to lunch."

She'd been weighed, asked to undress, probed by Stoner's cold fingers and then quickly dismissed with "Everything is perfect."

Cynthia hadn't known what to expect, so she'd expected the worst. She'd spent two weeks worrying, becoming progressively more on edge as this routine check-up approached. How was she supposed to know what would happen, what Stoner might find?

As soon as the appointment had been confirmed by Stoner's secretary, she'd started examining herself: gently touching the surface of the scar, feeling for irregularities, checking for bumps or changes in color. No one had told her what to look for, but she'd looked anyway.

As she walked out of Stoner's office, her body was still moist from the anticipatory beads of sweat she'd generated before and during the examination. She wondered whether it was always going to be like this, or whether, as time went on, this whole process would get easier. In actuality, though, this exam had been fairly simple and she was tremendously relieved.

She walked down the corridor to Meyer's office. She hadn't told him about the appointment but she had good news now and she wanted to share it.

She was disappointed when Betty told her that he had left the hospital to go out to lunch.

Cynthia took the elevator to the first floor and was heading toward the main entrance when she heard someone call out her name.

Ann Collins came up to her, smiling, her right hand extended in greeting. "Hi, Cynthia. How have you been?"

Cynthia, remembering Ann's warmth and help, took her hand.

"I've thought about you," Ann continued.

"I've been fine. How have you been?"

"Great . . . constantly tired, but that's the way it is around here. I'm on pediatrics now, taking care of little ones." She smiled. "I love it. It's a big change from surgery. What are you doing right now?" She didn't wait for a reply. "I've got exactly an hour for lunch. Come with me!"

Cynthia was caught up in Ann's enthusiasm. She nodded okay, and they headed out the doors and across the street to a hamburger palace.

Meyer leaned forward to answer Paul's question. "I have to make love to her. What's she going to think if I don't?" He paused and then answered his own question. "She'll think it's because she's deformed, because I don't find her appealing anymore."

Paul took a sip of his martini and said nothing.

"I feel tremendously pressured to have an orgasm every time we make love, sort of to validate the relationship. I'm afraid not to come."

Paul shook his head. "If you fail, it'll be because she's breaking your balls. How long are you going to put up with this? It seems to me that this relationship is causing you a lot more pain than happiness. I mean what good is it living with a girl you can hardly ever fuck, a girl who doesn't seem to want you around?"

"When do you have time for yourself, or anyone else?" Cynthia had become comfortable with Ann and suddenly she wanted to know all about her. Her initial resistance had been replaced by enthusiasm and she was really enjoying just sitting, eating a hamburger, talking and being out in the world.

"When I'm asleep," Ann laughed. "Becoming a doctor is a fabulous experience and I wouldn't trade it for anything, but medicine isn't conducive to having a normal sexy personal life."

"Do you want to get married?"

"I always wanted to get married and have lots of kids, but I got sidetracked. I kept having daydreams of myself dashing down a long corridor in a white coat, saving lives."

"That shouldn't stop you."

"I guess I've never had time to meet the right man. And, what kind of mother would I make, running around the hospital at all hours of the day and night?"

"I always wanted to marry, too . . ." Cynthia hesitated, "and have children. I guess I can't, now."

Ann looked at her. "Sure you can. I mean you shouldn't have a baby right away, because of the high estrogen levels during pregnancy, but after a few years, when everything is okay, there's no reason you can't have a child."

That seemed like a simple enough answer, but there was so much more to it. Cynthia hadn't made her point very well. For her, cancer was a terrible complication, but in an already complicated life. She had realized that her problems went back much further than the discovery of the growth in her breast. After her mother's death, she had become afraid to have children and she had begun to understand, only recently, that supporting this fear was her inability to have a serious relationship with a man. She didn't know where to begin or how much to say or even whether to discuss any of this at all with Ann.

"I'm not sure I'd make a very good mother," she finally said. "I didn't handle my operation very well and I really don't know if I could come through for my kids when they needed me."

Ann shook her head, realizing that they weren't really very dissimilar. "We're both scared," she said, "for different reasons, but we're both scared." She almost laughed. "We want the same things out of life and we both find excuses for not going after them, like my career and your operation; but you're doing fine. It takes some women a lot longer than this to even begin to get over a mastectomy. I really admire you."

Cynthia was surprised. She couldn't believe she'd elicited any admiration from a young woman who was breaking her butt, dedicating herself to becoming a doctor, and it made her happy.

"In five years," Ann said, "we'll be meeting in some sandbox."

They both laughed and ordered more coffee. Cynthia sat back and looked at Ann. "I've got a lot to tell you." She waited. "But first, I want to thank you."

Ann looked up. "What for?"

"For being the kind of person you are . . . for helping me when I was in the hospital; I never forgot you."

Paul paused until the waitress finished refilling his coffee cup and left, then he resumed speaking. "You've got to stop second-guessing yourself, Jon. What's done is done. It doesn't matter whether or not Cynthia would have responded better or differently to a partial mastectomy because there's no longer an opportunity to find out. You might not have cured her with a smaller operation."

"I don't know that she's cured now," Jon mumbled.

"If you did a smaller operation, how do you know that she wouldn't have developed some neurotic fear that you'd left cancer behind?" Paul didn't allow him to answer. "You don't! So you've got to stop this. You're driving yourself crazy and for no reason. It makes me sad to see you like this."

Paul reached across the table, taking his friend by the forearm. "I think you've got to get out, Jon." He waited for his words to sink in. "I think the world of Cynthia. I never met a woman I thought was more perfect for you. But things are different, now. None of this situation was your fault and you're acting as though it were. You're letting it destroy you. I think you've got to end the relationship. Bury yourself in the hospital. Get back to work. Break your ass! Become the old Jon, again. And let Cynthia and her psychiatrist work out Cynthia's problems."

24

It was almost 10:00 when the phone rang. Meyer had spent most of the evening in his study and had only just joined Cynthia in the living room.

"Dr. Meyer, hi, it's Steve Foley."

"Hi, Steve. What's up?"

"We just admitted a lady with appendicitis to your service."

"Appendicitis? What's she doing on my service? Why isn't she on general surgery?"

"Her name is Julia Featherton. She's one of the patients in the Breast Clinic."

"I don't know her," Meyer said.

"She's a white female, fifty-two years old. She had breast cancer seven years ago. She had a radical mastectomy with a couple of positive nodes and she received five thousand rads of X-ray therapy. We've seen her every six months for the past few years and everything has been fine.

"This afternoon, she developed vague periumbilical pain, lost her appetite and had some nausea. By seven the pain localized into the right lower quadrant of her abdomen, and she finally came into the hospital. Right now, she's got tenderness and rebound over McBurney's Point, a temp of 100.2 degrees and white blood count of fourteen thousand. It's classic."

"It certainly sounds like appendicitis," Meyer said. "Do you think it could be anything else?"

"I doubt it," Foley replied, "but we'll never know until we take a look."

"Let me warn you about a case like this," Meyer said. "It's probably appendicitis, but there's always a chance that a right colon cancer can be present with symptoms like these. Of course, a variety of gynecologic problems can show up this way, and if you want to reach for straws, a metastasis from her breast cancer could do this."

"Her pelvic is normal," Foley said, "and I can feel both of her ovaries. They're small and atrophic and I'm sure not the cause of her problem."

"Well," Meyer said, "there's no doubt that you've got to operate on her."

"I've already scheduled her," Foley replied. "I just wanted to let you know. There's no need for you to come in. I've told her that I'd be helping the junior resident and she's agreed."

"Thanks for calling, Steve. I'll be in shortly. Go ahead and start if I'm not there." Meyer hung up.

He was sure that Steve hadn't understood what had just happened on the phone. An appendectomy was a relatively minor surgical case, and in clinic patients, like Mrs. Featherton, the junior residents, with the help of a senior or chief resident, routinely did them while the staff man stayed home.

"I've got a case to do," Meyer told Cynthia.

She didn't ask any details and Meyer didn't volunteer any information.

The residents didn't need Meyer's help on an appendectomy, he knew that. He was going to the hospital because he was bored.

Twenty minutes after the call, he left the house.

As he drove along the freeway, he thought about the times when he was a resident. He could always tell what was going on in the personal life of a surgeon by how the surgeon reacted over the telephone to an emergency call and whether or not he was willing to come in and help him at night.

The miserably married surgeon or the one who was home by himself, bored and lonely, was always delighted to hear from the residents and he would come in for the slightest reason. The happily married man, who enjoyed his free time with his wife and kids, often resented being called, as though the emergency were the residents' fault. The single stud surgeon loved to come in when he had nothing to do and he hated to be called when he was trying to get laid. But if he had just fucked someone, he always appreciated an emergency, it made him look like a hero and it gave him an excuse to leave in a hurry.

Steve Foley was a happily married man and Meyer seriously doubted that he had ever consciously constructed these various scenarios.

When he arrived at the hospital, Meyer went directly to the operating suite and changed into surgical greens. Mrs. Featherton was just arriving so he lay down on one of the couches in the doctors' dressing room.

Steve Foley came in moments later. "Hi, you didn't have to come in for this case."

"I know," Meyer replied. "I just wanted to get out of the house for a few hours." He wanted to reassure him. "I have absolute confidence in you."

Mrs. Featherton was groggy from the premedication, but still awake. Meyer took her hand and introduced himself. He examined her gently, talking to her, trying to set her mind at ease.

It was after 12:00 when the case finally got started. Steve Foley directed the junior resident to make an up and down incision rather than a transverse one over the appendix. His reasoning was sound. Even though this appeared to be a straightforward case of appendicitis, the lady was fifty-two years old and had previously had cancer. The residents had to be prepared to find something else, and if they did, this incision would allow them better exposure.

Meyer didn't bother to scrub. At first, he'd sat in the corner of the room, out of the way, while they'd draped. Then he'd moved up closer, looking over Steve Foley's shoulder.

They cut through the skin, the fat and the hard fibrous fascia before reaching the muscle. They freed the muscle and retracted it to the right. The bleeding was minimal and easily controlled with the electrocautery.

They opened the fascia behind the rectus muscle. The junior resident asked for the toothed forceps and they were placed in his hand; the other pair was automatically given to Foley.

The younger resident carefully picked up the peritoneum, Foley helping by grasping it opposite him. He proceeded to make a small opening into the abdominal cavity.

"You're in," Foley announced.

The junior resident enlarged the incision and, as he did, a loop of small bowel popped out. He pushed it back in and another one popped out.

"Would you relax the patient?" he said impatiently to the anesthesiologist.

"Just a second," the anesthesiologist muttered.

The junior resident waited for the relaxation. He was on edge.

Meyer looked across the table at him. He knew how he felt. He'd been in the same place fifteen years ago.

"Let's go," Foley said. "She's relaxed now."

They placed a couple of retractors into the abdomen and began looking around. As they pushed the small bowel out of the way, they saw it, a red, inflamed appendix. She clearly had appendicitis and, most likely, nothing more.

If they had taken out the appendix and failed to look any further in a patient who had a history of cancer, Meyer would have been disappointed.

After the appendix was removed and the acute disease process cured, the junior resident asked for an O-chromic to begin closing.

"Is that all you want to do?" Foley asked.

"Sure," the junior resident said, "unless you want me to take out her gall bladder." He laughed.

"A simple appendectomy is not enough," Foley said. "She's had cancer and she's probably cured, but while you're here you ought to make certain. There's no test you can order upstairs that'll give you as good a look in her belly as the one you're getting right now. So before you close look around a bit."

With that, Meyer was satisfied. He would be happy to send Steve Foley out into the community.

"I'm going to go up to 6-North for some coffee," he said. "If you find anything else, let me know."

The elevator made an abrupt stop on the second floor. As the door opened, a familiar face entered. It was Joan.

She smiled. "Hi, Jon. What are you doing here in the middle of the night?"

"I came in to watch the boys do a case."

"Who did you operate on?"

"Oh, a lady named Featherton. We took out her appendix."

"Since when do you come in for appendicitis?"

"Whenever I feel like having coffee with you"—Meyer looked at his watch—"at one in the morning."

The elevator door opened and they were on 6-North.

"Come on down to the nurses' station," she said, "I'll buy."

Meyer smiled. The coffee was free but it was still a good offer.

Joan was about thirty-two years old, married when she was twenty-one, divorced five years later and without children. She had been a nurse for a long time, perhaps ten or twelve years, and she was good at it.

She and Meyer had developed a special understanding for each other without really knowing very much about one another. Joan was the only nurse on the floor who called Meyer by his first name.

Joan was the nurse who, five months ago, had said to

Meyer, "Your lady wore too much of her personality on her chest. Now half of it's gone." And she was clearly aware that he was suffering increasing pain.

"Mrs. Featherton is a Breast Clinic patient," Meyer said as he sipped his coffee, "so I thought I'd come in and take a peek."

Joan looked into Meyer's eyes and shook her head slowly. "Bullshit, Jon. Your residents know how to take out an appendix."

"Yes, but I don't," he said with a smile. "I haven't taken one out for years."

She laughed and changed the subject, knowing she wasn't really changing it. "Are you still living with your lady . . . Cynthia?"

Meyer nodded yes.

"How's it going?"

"Poorly."

"I know where you're at," Joan said. "I've known for some time."

"How do you know?" Meyer asked, although he did believe that she knew.

"All I have to do is to look at you, Jon . . . at your face . . . and I can tell. I watch the way you walk, listen to what you say, watch how you relate to the nurses, to the patients. I watch you teach. I can tell. You haven't been happy for a long time and that makes me sad."

Meyer didn't deny it. He just looked at her. Then he began telling her everything. She was the first real outsider that he'd ever talked to about Cynthia. He desperately needed to relate the story to someone, someone completely detached from him, someone objective.

Joan was small with a very feminine body, short blond hair and a roundish almost pixie-like face. She looked at least ten years younger than she was. She listened attentively to Meyer, and when he was through she offered no advice.

Finally, she glanced at her watch. "I've got to get back to work." She began to walk out of the room.

"Thanks for listening," Meyer called out.

She stopped, smiled and walked back toward him. Leaning over, she kissed him on the forehead. "You're okay, Meyer."

She started out the door, stopped again, turned and came back into the room. She rested her hand on his shoulder. "Let's have breakfast together. I think it's about time."

"I have to go home," Meyer said.

"No, you don't. Do you want to have breakfast with me?"

"Yes," he answered.

She reached into her uniform pocket and pulled out a ring of keys. She slipped one off. "It's apartment 201." She wrote the address on a slip of paper. "I'll be home by a quarter to eight." Then she left.

Meyer stayed to think. Before he was married, he'd had multiple girl friends. Occasionally, when he did settle into a relationship, he had trouble being faithful. In fact, he never was.

During the early part of his marriage, he'd felt trapped and he'd taken up with a number of previous lovers but he'd never felt guilty.

When Nancy and he finally decided to get a divorce,

they still had six months left in their residencies and they decided to continue living together. Occasionally they made love, and sporadically they dated other people.

Those were probably the best six months of the entire marriage. They became good friends during those months and Meyer actually began to feel some guilt and pain. But it wasn't related to his outside affairs. Rather, it was the sadness he felt as a friend having to part. It was guilt generated by the fact maybe he hadn't tried hard enough or when he'd finally begun trying it was too late.

But now, for the first time in his life, Meyer felt guilty about what he was contemplating. Not only had he not cheated since he'd met Cynthia, he hadn't even looked at another woman. He'd had no outside sexual thoughts despite how badly things were going at home. He had been totally faithful and he was proud of it.

Maybe Joan and he wouldn't make love. Maybe they would just have breakfast. No, that was ridiculous. They had waited years for the combination of circumstances that would make it right and this was obviously it.

As he drove toward Joan's apartment, Meyer realized that, inside, he hadn't changed a great deal in the last twenty years.

He'd gone through three phases in his life and basically they were all the same. When he was younger, all he'd cared about was basketball. Winning games and scoring points were all that had mattered to him.

When he'd finally gotten interested in girls, he'd counted them instead of baskets.

As a doctor, he'd remained the same ferocious competitor he'd always been. Only now he kept score with the lives he saved, the papers he wrote, the number of students he taught and the amount of grant money he raised.

His thoughts saddened him. The game he played was the same; only the stakes had changed.

He parked his car on a side street, although he was certain that no one would be looking for it. He left the front door unlocked so that Joan would be able to get in when she got home and he called the hospital operator telling her that he'd be on the beeper all night and not to call him at home.

He took off his clothes, piled them neatly on a chair in a corner, took a shower and went to bed.

He fell asleep as soon as his head hit the pillow. He didn't bother to run the guilt trip through his mind another time.

He woke up when he heard the shower running. His beeper was next to the bed and it hadn't gone off. He called the hospital to make sure. It was a new day and there were new operators on duty. There were no messages. No one had called and he felt protected. He looked over at the clock. It was five minutes of eight.

The bathroom door opened and Joan came out, a towel wrapped completely around her.

"Me or breakfast first?"

"You," he said.

"Good." She smiled.

"I've got to brush my teeth," Meyer said.

"Be my guest."

Joan waited in bed. When he crawled back under the covers, they were immediately in each other's arms. It was wild and animalistic. There were no words. They knew what to do to one another and they did it.

Joan fell asleep in his arms.

Minutes later, Meyer slipped out of bed, dressed and left.

It was Saturday morning. He picked up the residents at about 9:30 as they were finishing rounds. He lengthened rounds by about thirty minutes with some good, inspired teaching. As they finished and the residents went their separate ways, his beeper went off. He picked up the wall phone and dialed the operator.

"I have an outside call, Dr. Meyer, from Miss Rogers."

"I'll take it, operator, and thank you. . . . Good morning," he said cheerfully.

"Where have you been?" Cynthia asked.

"I've been at the hospital all night, doing a case . . ."

"I woke up in the middle of the night," she said, "and you weren't back and I was afraid. So I called the operating room, but they said that you'd left just after one."

"I did, but I was tired, so I went to sleep on my couch. Besides, I had to make rounds this morning, so it was simpler to stay. Any time something like that happens, all you have to do is to ask the operator to beep me. She can usually find me."

"Oh," she said and she seemed satisfied. "When are you coming home?"

"Well, grand rounds just started and they'll be done by eleven-thirty, so I'll be home by about twelve-thirty. Can I bring you anything?"

"I'd love to go out today." She sounded enthusiastic.

"Maybe we could eat at one of the little places on the beach."

"That would be fine," Jon said and he hung up.

He couldn't believe it. He'd cheated one time after five months of absolute faithfulness and he'd almost gotten caught. Maybe he wanted to get caught. It would certainly shake up the relationship. Maybe it would get better or maybe it would end. Either way, he thought, would be more acceptable than the way it was now.

He wondered what Cynthia would do if she caught him cheating. It would probably be the last thing in the world that she'd want to find out. It would simply confirm that their relationship was failing and she would, of course, interpret it to mean that he no longer found her appealing in any way. But that was something, he was sure, she wouldn't want to find out. It would be much too painful. He was certain that she'd bury her head in the sand for as long as possible. She would be far blinder than the average woman.

He knew he was still attracted to her body. Her mastectomy hadn't made him cheat. He just couldn't seem to stand the whole experience any longer. He couldn't stand being closed out.

He walked into grand rounds and sat down. It had already begun and one of his residents was presenting the case. It was a cancer patient and the resident knew the material absolutely cold. Most of what he was saying were things that Meyer had taught him. As Meyer listened, he forgot about his own problems. Medicine had always been the best medicine for him.

25

Cynthia went directly to the ladies' room on the first floor of the Neuropsychiatric Institute. She hoped no one else would come in for the next few minutes. There were three toilets and she automatically chose the last one, the one farthest from the door.

She bolted the stall door and laid her large canvas bag down on the cold tile floor. She slipped off her skirt and blouse and hung them on the hook instead of folding them and neatly putting them into her bag.

Feeling chilly and exposed, she quickly pulled out her leotards and tights. She sat down on the seat of the toilet —there was no lid—and slipped off her shoes. She stuck her feet into the stocking portion of her tights and stood up, stretching the black elastic material over her long legs as she rose.

Next, stepping through the V neckline of her leotard, she pulled it up quickly, inserting her arms through the tight sleeves. As she covered her chest and shoulders, she was relieved.

She grabbed her dancing shoes, put them on and then, when she was completely dressed, she took the time to fold her street clothes and put them away.

Unlocking the stall door, she peered out, making certain no one else had come into the bathroom. She went over to the mirror above the sinks. She was dissatisfied, it just didn't look right. She could see the edge of her bra protruding out between the V neckline, and when she looked carefully she could perceive the lack of a bulge where her breast used to be.

Somehow, it hadn't seemed this bad when she'd tried it on at home and she worried whether the children might notice, whether it might upset them.

She reached into her canvas bag and took out a safety pin. She pulled the lower portion of the V neck together, pinning it. It was better, but it still wasn't quite right.

She glanced toward the door, still hoping no one would come in. She slipped the right side of the leotard off over her shoulder and adjusted the prosthesis. Finally, she was ready.

She'd decided not to tell any of the doctors at the institute what had happened to her. She was afraid that if they knew they might not have allowed her to return to work.

Cynthia walked down the hall and into the therapy room. The children were already there, waiting for her. Those who remembered her were happy to see her and they came running up to hug her. She reached out, pulling two of them close to her. A third one pushed his way into her arms, as though he were a hungry puppy. She was touched by their warmth and their unhesitating acceptance of her.

"I want you to know," she said, "this is a very special day for me."

26

"*Now that I'm* back at work, I don't have to devote all my time to thinking about myself and the loss of my breast. But I am worried that the children will notice something different and it will upset them."

"Do you really think they'll notice?" Anna asked. "Maybe we should talk about how *you* feel."

"I'm sick of talking about myself."

"If you'd rather not think about yourself now, how about the person closest to you? How does Jon feel about your returning to work?"

"I don't know, I haven't told him."

"Don't you think that he'd be pleased to know that you've made this step forward?"

"Yes, I guess he would, but we haven't been talking much lately, he doesn't have any time. He's very busy."

"Too busy for you to tell him how you are feeling and what you are doing? Is that the way you want it?"

"I don't know what I want. I don't know what Jon wants either. Sometimes I'm afraid that as I improve he withdraws more and more from me. At first, after the operation, I was afraid he was going to reject me because I had so many problems. Now that I'm getting better, I'm afraid that he'll reject me because I won't seem to need him anymore."

Anna leaned forward. "Well, that brings up several thoughts in my mind." She waited a moment until she had Cynthia's full attention. "Who else rejected you?"

Cynthia looked at Anna and shrugged. "Lots of people."

"Your mother and your father," Anna said softly.

"My mother didn't reject me. She loved me."

"But she did die and any young person can feel or interpret that as a form of rejection. After all, where is she now when you need her the most, or for that matter, where was she before, when you were growing up?"

Cynthia looked away from Anna. "Maybe you're right." She paused. "I do miss her so much. I've always missed her. I never understood why she had to die."

"We will be spending a lot more time talking about that."

"But I know it wasn't her fault," Cynthia added quickly.

Anna nodded. "Let's continue in the direction we've started. What about your father?"

"What about him?"

"He buried himself in his grief and work after your mother died. Isn't that what you've said before? That he rejected you?"

"Yes, that sounds like something I would have said." Cynthia smiled awkwardly. "I guess I've complained a lot about my father not really caring about me. He gave me everything—except himself."

"Now you are living with someone. In the beginning, you depended on your good looks and your gay personality rather than what was inside of you. You couldn't fool yourself and you assumed that, ultimately, Jon would tire of that façade and reject you. Then, when this crisis arose and you had your breast removed, as you just stated, you were afraid he would reject you because you had so many new problems. But he didn't reject you then, either. Now you are improving and you say that Jon will recognize this healthier attitude and reject you because you won't appear to need him anymore. You seem always to be searching for a reason for failure. Perhaps if Jon does end the relationship, it will be his problem and not yours." Anna waited for all this to sink in. "Have you thought about his side to all of this?"

"No, I guess I haven't. I've been too wrapped up in myself."

"When you are in the middle of a relationship, it's often difficult to see and evaluate the other person objectively. I can only tell you how I evaluate it and you should think about it. Jon is clearly a highly regulated and self-sufficient man. He doesn't need anyone. Yet he obviously cares a great deal for people and he certainly showed that he cared about you. However, after your operation, Jon brought home a patient, not a woman or a lover—a patient—for him, a crippled child.

"Jon is at his best caring for people who need him when they are sick, when he can play the role of healer. Now, all of a sudden, he is discovering that he is living with a human being, a woman who is becoming healthier every day, a woman who is curing herself. You are challenging some of those unused portions of his personality, the internal parts of him that need someone. He has to learn to give and take on a personal level and I wonder if that is threatening to him."

"Do you think he really wants a relationship with me?" Cynthia asked.

"I don't know. Do you want to find out?"

Cynthia sat back in her chair. She had to answer that question.

When Cynthia came into the study, Jon was looking through a book and seemed very engrossed in it.

"May I come in?"

Jon looked up. "Sure, but I have to finish this for a lecture tomorrow."

Cynthia took the chair opposite Jon's desk, pulled it closer to him and sat down.

"I saw Anna today."

"Don't you see her every day?"

"No, Jon, not every day." She paused. "We talked about something I thought you and I should discuss. We talked a lot about you." She smiled, hoping not to make him defensive, or feel that she'd invaded his privacy.

"Is that what you spend your sessions talking about? Me?" He wondered whether she'd found out about Joan or if she suspected. Maybe it would be better if they talked about it.

"Of course not," she said. "We talk about lots of things. I'm living with you and we don't spend much time together. The little we do spend with one another isn't very good anymore."

"Do you think that's my fault?"

"No, I'm not blaming you. Most of the problem lies

with me. I haven't been very easy to live with. But I'm trying to think more of you now. What I really need to know is what you want from me, from our relationship."

He didn't have a quick answer. He felt ambivalent. He had wanted to love Cynthia, but so much had happened to keep them apart. He closed the book before saying anything. "I don't know what I want." He was frustrated at not having a decent response.

"Have you been thinking about it?" she asked.

"Not really." That wasn't true. He knew he thought about it all the time. But over the last few months everything had come to seem hopeless.

"Then there's not much point in my telling you what I want," she said.

"No, go ahead, tell me if you'd like to."

Cynthia stood up. "I don't want to tell you just because you're listening at the moment. I want to tell you when you want to hear it, when you care!"

"How will I know when you've decided that I'm ready?" Jon raised his voice. "I don't usually have other people telling me how to feel."

"I know. You're a very self-sufficient man. Maybe you don't need anyone, ever!"

Jon sat back. This was the first angry interaction they'd had in a long time. He was surprised, almost happy.

27

"*Dammit, Cynthia, why* didn't you tell me before? I'm hurt, really hurt. What good are friends if you don't let them comfort you when you need them?"

"I guess I just didn't trust anyone enough to let them in, to ask for help."

"Well, your father would never have forgiven me, and I'll never forgive you." Alice Stern put her hand on Cynthia's arm. "I forgive you, darling . . . but give me a break now," she pleaded. "What can I do for you? How have you been? Are you all right?"

Alice wanted to know everything and, to Cynthia's surprise, she was warm, loving, caring and everything else that Cynthia could possibly ask for in a friend.

Suddenly, Alice stood up. There were tears in her eyes and she bent over and hugged Cynthia to her. "We've got to get you back to living a normal life again. Everyone at the club misses you. I missed you; I didn't think you wanted to see me." She sat down. "Maybe I should have tried harder to find out."

Cynthia shook her head. "No, I was hidden away, wrapped up in self-pity and I didn't want to share that with anyone. You couldn't have gotten through to me even if you had tried. Thanks, anyway."

"What about Jon? Are you still with him?"

"I'm with him, but we're not really together. We're having a lot of problems."

"Where is he tonight?"

"I don't know, probably at the hospital. His way of dealing with things is to bury himself in his work."

"Well," Alice said, "I think you're incredibly brave to want to go to Logos for a drink. Why do you want to go? It's such a conspicuous contemptuous place."

"I want to go because I have to get back into life. I have to meet other people and at least try to cope with some of the old familiar scenes."

"Well, I'm going with you as counsel and bodyguard." Alice laughed.

The plush brown and beige velvet couches were comfortable enough but the low lighting and the loud music made conversation almost impossible. It was relatively early so they had no trouble finding a little corner to sit in while they watched the few dancers who had already begun to gyrate for the evening.

Alice was having a fine time watching the young blonds and their white-haired male companions. She carefully checked out everyone's attire, continually commenting on which shops their outfits had been purchased from. She even got Cynthia to laugh a few times with her snide remarks.

Several people who knew Cynthia, and some who were

just attracted to her, nodded their hellos and smiled at her. Some asked her to dance, but she declined.

Around 11:00, still very early for a Logos evening, a somewhat attractive man in his early forties came over to their couch area and sat down. He wanted to start a conversation with Cynthia, even though she had refused to dance.

Alice tried to pretend that she was watching the dancers. She didn't want to intrude, but she couldn't resist eavesdropping.

"You have beautiful eyes," he said and Cynthia smiled. It had been a long time since someone had really tried to pick her up. "Haven't I seen you here before?" He answered his own question: "I wouldn't have forgotten you, you're the prettiest girl here." He grinned.

"Thank you."

"Listen, it's very hard to hear in here, do you want to go out to the bar? I'll buy you a drink."

"I don't think so. I really should stay with my friend."

He glanced over at Alice. "Oh, she's having a fine time." Then he turned toward Alice. "You wouldn't mind if I took your pretty friend out for a drink, now would you?" he asked in a loud voice.

Alice wasn't sure what Cynthia wanted her to do, so she just shrugged her shoulders.

Cynthia smiled and shook her head, no. "I'd rather stay here. Thank you, though."

The man decided to get bolder. "Well, if you don't come and have a drink with me now, how about going home with me later?" He laid his hand on her knee and smiled broadly.

She looked directly at him. "I want you to know something . . . I've had a mastectomy."

Alice couldn't believe her ears.

"I beg your pardon?" He wasn't sure what she'd said.

"I've had a mastectomy. . . . I only have one breast. I don't know how you feel about that."

He didn't know how he felt either, that was obvious, because he became very flustered, changing the subject and ultimately excusing himself, saying that he'd forgotten that he had friends waiting for him.

Cynthia drove Alice home. "I didn't mean to shock him. But I think it was harder for me to say than for him to hear."

"Why did you tell him?"

"I just felt like saying it. Anyone who wants to know me is going to have to know sooner or later. I'll just have to work it out." She thought for a few moments. "Maybe there's a better way."

Suddenly, Cynthia pulled over to the side of the road. She stopped the engine and looked at Alice. Tears welled up in her eyes and she began to cry. Alice hugged her.

"I've got a long way to go."

"Well, I think you're doing fine, just slow down."

28

Meyer made it to Joan's apartment by twenty after seven. He hadn't told any of his friends about his affair. He was certain that neither Paul nor Susan would have approved, regardless of his needs or his reasons. Paul would have used it as ammunition to suggest again that he terminate the relationship with Cynthia; and Susan would have been terribly disappointed in him.

Meyer glanced at his watch as he came into the apartment.

Joan looked crossly at him. "You never have any time, do you?"

A week ago she had started making requests for his time, and although they were minimal, they were still demands, and in Meyer's mind any demands would quickly prove to be intolerable.

"I'm sorry," he said.

"What good does that do me? I want some sort of relationship. I want someone I can talk to, spend a little time with." She shrugged her shoulders. "I guess I want someone who can take me to the movies or out to dinner once in a while."

Meyer looked at her. She was absolutely right. The relationship had no potential and they both knew it. Yet, in Meyer's experience, most women were unable to break off relationships like this one. Because as bad as they were, there usually wasn't anyone available who was better.

Joan's only way out was if she found someone else, someone more appropriate, someone who wasn't "married."

All Meyer had to do, however, to abort this terminal process was to smile at her, to say that he was sorry, that he would change, that things would be different. He could rub her neck, smooth her hair out, kiss her and hold her and everything would be fine.

He shook his head. "This relationship is no good for you and it's no good for me."

She was surprised.

"I can't give you anything," he continued. "I can only hurt you."

She stared at him, not believing the little she had said had triggered this absolute response.

"I've felt like this from the beginning," he said. "I'm glad you brought it up. If you hadn't then I would have, if not tonight, then the next time we were together."

It was just after eight o'clock when Meyer arrived home. Cynthia was in the living room reading.

"I thought you were going to be home late," she said. "Did you eat yet?"

"No."

"I could fix you something." She got up.

"That would be nice."

"It's good that you came home early. I'd like to talk with you. I have a lot to tell you."

"Okay, let me take a quick shower and change."

As he washed his body, Jon was glad that he hadn't gone to bed with Joan.

They sat in front of the fireplace. He ate and she told him her news.

For several weeks now, she'd been teaching again and there were no problems. The children were happy to see her and she was glad to be back, working.

She had met with Alice, confided in her and Alice had come through. She had made a mistake by not taking Alice into her confidence earlier, giving her a chance to be a friend.

And finally Cynthia produced the pink registration card. She had signed up for school and she would begin to finish college and get her degree.

Meyer was delighted and he opened a bottle of wine to celebrate. They sat by the fire and talked for another hour. He took her hand and held it.

They went into the bedroom and, without speaking, they began to undress one another.

She stood in front of him in her bra and underpants. He looked at the fleshy fullness of her left breast and he looked at the silicone prosthesis that filled the right side.

He reached behind her, unhooked the bra and removed it with the prosthesis in place.

He kissed the erect nipple of her one perfect breast. He looked at the flatness where there had once been a gentle curve and he kissed her right chest.

He pulled her closer, kissing her lips, then holding her.

Then she stood naked in front of him and he ran his hands over her body. She was beautiful.

They made love, and to Meyer it became clear that everything was going to be all right. He told Cynthia that, and he slept well that night.

29

Jon drove swiftly in the far left lane of the freeway. He was looking forward to his day at the hospital and he was also looking forward to going home, to being with Cynthia again.

He made rounds and headed to the operating room to help one of his residents with a case.

Cynthia had gotten up just after Jon had left. She'd slept very poorly and had finally reached a decision.

She showered, dressed and pulled her two suitcases down from the closet. She started packing.

It was 10:20 when one of Meyer's residents came into the operating room to give him a message.

"A patient of yours, Mr. Baum, the fellow you did a Whipple on about six months ago . . ."

"Yes," Meyer said through his mask.

"He's in the emergency room. He had a grand mal seizure earlier this morning. He's unconscious, having a lot of trouble breathing."

"Who's with him?" Meyer asked.

"Foley and Margolies."

"Fine, go back and help them. Tell Foley that I'll be there as soon as I can and tell him to call a neurosurgeon."

About thirty minutes later, as soon as it was technically possible, Meyer left the operating room. He slipped on a long white coat over his green scrub suit and headed directly for the emergency room.

He'd just seen Mr. Baum three weeks ago and he'd been in perfect shape, not a sign of trouble. Two possibilities went through Meyer's mind: the first, a brain tumor, probably metastatic from Baum's pancreatic cancer; the second, a cerebrovascular accident, a stroke of some sort.

He found Foley and two of his other residents in the hall outside room number seven.

"Dr. Rosenberg is in with him," Foley said. "We had to put an endotracheal tube in and put him on a positive pressure respirator. He stopped breathing."

Meyer went directly into the room. The neurosurgeon stopped momentarily, acknowledging Meyer's presence, and then continued his examination. He turned the lights down in the room and with his ophthalmoscope looked deeply into Baum's right eye. He walked quickly around the table and then looked into the left.

He flipped on the lights and began talking to Meyer. "He's got four-plus papilledema on both sides and a left hemiparesis. I think he's got a space occupying lesion in the right temporoparietal region. I'd start dehydrating him right now with mannitol and steroids, get some of the fluid out of his brain and relieve the pressure, then scan his brain. If that doesn't show it, we can do an arteriogram." He looked at Meyer. "I doubt that he has much of a chance. I disconnected him from the respirator and he was completely apneic, not even an agonal respiration."

Meyer shook his head. "I saw him a few weeks ago. He was fine."

Rosenberg shrugged his shoulders. "The tumor just took some time to get big enough to cause symptoms."

Foley, who had been listening to the conversation, turned to the nurse and ordered four milligrams of Decadron intravenously and 250 c.c.s of mannitol.

"We can give him whole brain irradiation, maybe shrink the tumor," Meyer said. "That's about his only chance."

"And then what have you got?" Rosenberg answered his own question: "A man who is paralyzed, who probably can't talk, has pancreatic cancer metastatic to his brain and God knows where else and who is accumulating a bigger hospital bill."

"We've got to try," Meyer said.

"Why?" Rosenberg asked.

Cynthia carried the second suitcase into her apartment. It was hot and stuffy, the air smelled foul. She opened all the windows, changed into her jeans and went downstairs to get one of the large green garbage cans.

She carried it into the living room and she began cleaning, throwing away dead plant after dead plant.

She had to do what she did, she thought. She had to leave. He had simply missed the point. He had measured her responses, her health, her well-being and, most of all, their relationship in terms of things, external things, external accomplishments. Getting a job, going back to school, love-making: in his mind they all proved that she was well, that they were going to be all right, that there would be no other problems. Well, that just wasn't the answer for her. There was much more to it.

She had healed inside, but not completely, maybe never completely, but she knew she had progressed. He had been blind to her improvement until he had tangible evidence that he could use as a measuring stick. And that was wrong!

She could not be with him unless he made the kind of progress that she was making. He had to grow from within. He had to become a whole person and it was nothing that could be measured or scored. It had to be a process of internal emotional growth for him. She hoped he could do it because she could settle for nothing less.

The brain scan was absolute. There were three easily seen large metastases in Baum's brain and, most likely, dozens of others. An arteriogram would be traumatic and unnecessary.

Meyer carefully explained the situation to Mrs. Baum. And he explained their only chance: radical X-ray therapy to Mr. Baum's whole brain. His hair would fall out and there would be all the other side effects of X-ray therapy; it would be given daily for the next two to three weeks. It was their only hope.

Mrs. Baum looked back at Meyer and she shook her head. "No," she answered.

A while ago, the Baums had talked and they had played out a scene vaguely like this one. They had both agreed. They were thankful for whatever extra time Meyer had given them, but when the end came there would be no heroics. Anyway, this had been a particularly merciful end. There had been no suffering. Aside from a slight headache for the past week, Mr. Baum had been perfectly well until 9:15 that morning; he knew nothing further after the seizure.

Meyer and Mrs. Baum sat in the small family room on 6-North. She told him about their life together and she convinced him that nothing further should be done. Mr. Baum died at 3:20 P.M.

Meyer had been in the room when it had happened. He'd watched Mrs. Baum as she'd held her husband. The cardiac monitor was flat. Meyer had put his arms around her and ushered her out of the room as the nurses began disconnecting the electronic equipment from the still body.

She'd turned, put her arms around Meyer and cried. It had happened so quickly, their children hadn't even had time to come to Los Angeles.

Cynthia sat in the one room Jon had never seen, her private workroom. The door to the hall and the windows were wide open, a fresh ocean breeze blowing in. The trash can was partially filled with dried, useless paints, ruined old dirty brushes and cloths and a canvas she'd started but had never finished.

She had placed a new canvas on the easel, deciding that she would go to the art supply shop in the morning, get whatever she needed and start a new painting.

She walked over to the exercise barre, gripping it with both hands. She lifted her leg up and out to the side until it was almost parallel with the barre. She smiled as she looked at her dirty face in the wall-length mirror. She was covered with dust and sweat from a full day's cleaning.

She knew she hadn't left Jon just to challenge him. She had to get back into her own life, redeem the best parts of herself. She needed to share what she was, not just live in Jon's world and take from him. She was proud of what she was and how she'd dealt with what she'd been through. She could have done better, but it didn't matter now, she'd handled it. She was becoming a whole person. She wanted to be half of any relationship and she was ready to contribute her half. If Jon wanted a relationship with her, he would have to begin sharing some of her life.

Meyer felt terribly sad. His eyes were wet as he walked slowly back to his office. He couldn't understand why he was quite so moved by this particular death. He'd spent years hardening himself and he'd never cried before for a patient. He'd been sad, but he'd never cried.

He'd hated death when he was a medical student, never really getting over his childhood fear of it. When he was a sophomore, taking pathology, he had gotten closer to it than ever before.

As a freshman, he'd dissected a cadaver while taking anatomy, but that had turned out to be nothing compared with pathology. The cadaver was hardly human, it was preserved, its blood drained, its nerves, arteries, veins all looking almost the same.

But in pathology he'd been forced to help with the postmortem examination of patients who had recently died. Often their bodies were still warm and their blood dark red. The autopsy room always smelled of death, a combination of blood, feces and bacteria.

He had hated pathology, and if he had ever thought of quitting medical school, it was while taking that course. At first he'd become nauseated in the morgue, but he'd continually forced himself to come back, to participate in autopsies.

For two straight months during lunch hours, at the end of the day, between classes, whenever possible, he went to the morgue. He touched death, he looked at it, he dissected it. He found scientific ways to explain it. He played games with it. He looked for clues. He learned to dissociate life from death, mind from body and, gradually, he got used to it.

He was incredibly sad as he sat in his office. He looked at his watch; it was only 4:00. He picked up the phone and buzzed Betty. "Tell the residents to make rounds without me. If Dr. Foley needs me, I'll be on the beeper."

He was upset when he didn't see Cynthia's car in the driveway. He needed to talk with her, to share with her what had happened to him during the day. He went inside and discovered that her suitcases and all her clothes were gone. He finally went into the study and found the note she'd left for him. He read it:

> *Dear Jon,*
>   *Imagine . . . if* you *had lost an eye.*
>   *Cynthia*

He sat back in his chair, rereading the note. He understood completely. He folded it carefully. Leaning forward, he opened the small carved wooden box on the front corner of his desk. He slipped in Cynthia's note, hesitated and then took out a slightly larger folded sheet of paper. He sat back again, unfolded the poem he'd written over a year ago and read it:

> *For the last eight years of my life*
> *I have worked only with cancer patients*
> *I have watched them waste away and die*
> *I have seen their last desperate moments*
> *I have felt the loneliness when they die alone*
> *I have seen the value of a family*
> *The richness of love*
> *The meaning when one person deeply cares for you*
> *I have seen my own emptiness*

He had felt almost like that again today. He had written that poem in a moment of sadness when he wasn't capable of doing anything about his feelings. But those were old feelings now. He smiled, crumpling up the poem and throwing it into the wastebasket.

He got into his car and headed for Cynthia's apartment.